The Highbury Murders

A Mystery Set in the Village of Jane Austen's *Emma*

Victoria Grossack

ISBN: 1482627450
ISBN-13: 978-1482627459

FOR CATHERINE,

who took care of me when I was injured and who loves a good cup of tea

CONTENTS

ACKNOWLEDGMENTS

I must thank Catherine Cresswell, for her advice about
agriculture in Surrey, Alice Underwood
for her assistance with formatting and cover design,
and Debbie Chambers and Susan Warren,
who both have sharp eyes and
who both made many helpful suggestions.

© Chrislofoto | Stock Free Images
& Dreamstime Stock Photos
is the source of the cover photo.

Jane Austen,
though long dead, remains a great inspiration.

1 CONDOLENCE CALLS IN THE BATES APARTMENT

The death of Mrs. Bates, a very old lady whose hearing had long since gone and who had spent her last few months either in her bedroom or sitting in her chair in the parlor, would have gone unremarked in London, where people spent their time discussing fashion, nobility, and the latest offering at the theatre. In Bath her decease might have been mentioned as a piece of dull news, before the residents and visitors resumed discussing who had been seen at the Pump Room during the day or who was giving a whist party that night. In Highbury, however, Mrs. Bates's passing was an event which was talked over in every house, both great and small. They wondered about her last hours, hoped that their own ends would be so peaceful, and discussed what they had heard about the funeral arrangements. To the romantic, a death may not hold the same fascination as the hopes for a wedding, but just as young ones begin, old lives must end.

As soon as it was deemed that the undertaker had done what was necessary, and that the nearest and dearest were ready for it, those who claimed any acquaintance with the Bates family – and that was most of the parish, as Mrs. Bates was the widow of a former, fondly remembered vicar of Highbury – entered through the door shared with the shop below, climbed the dark and narrow staircase, turned at the landing, and crowded into the tiny apartment to offer their condolences to Miss Bates.

Miss Bates was the middle-aged spinster daughter of the just deceased Mrs. Bates, and she received the visits of friends and neighbors with a voluble mixture of gratitude and sorrow. "Mrs. Knightley, you are so kind and yes, we – I mean I, after so many years with my dear mother I cannot yet learn to say I, but I know she would be as thankful for your words as

1

well, so perhaps the word we is appropriate"-- wiping away a tear, but smiling at the same time – "we were so grateful too for the lovely note sent earlier by your kind father, Mr. Woodhouse! So considerate of him! I have received notes from so many people; I am quite overwhelmed! The Coles sent over this cake, may I offer you a piece? And Mr. and Mrs. Weston have brought a large cheese, and the Perrys have been so kind as to send a bottle of wine to drink to my mother's spirit, would you care for a glass, Mrs. Knightley? My mother would be so honored."

Mrs. Emma Knightley, daughter of Mr. Woodhouse, the wealthiest man in the parish of Highbury, and also happily the wife of Mr. George Knightley, the local magistrate, farmer and the owner of the estate known as Donwell Abbey, in the adjacent parish, was the most recent to squeeze into the apartment, which was already full of Westons, Eltons and Coles. Emma took advantage of Miss Bates's pausing for breath to accept a tiny glass of wine and to say what else needed to be said. "My husband will call upon you later, but he asked me to tell you that he grieves for you. Also, he is honored to serve as one of your mother's pallbearers."

"Ah, thank you, that is so kind of him – Mother would be so grateful, and of course Mr. Knightley must be terribly busy with the harvest. Time and tide wait for no man, and nor do the apples and the onions – nor death," and Miss Bates sighed and looked at Mrs. Bates's chair in the corner, which was vacant out of respect for the deceased, even though every other seat was filled and some of the gentlemen were obliged to stand. Mrs. Emma Knightley had accepted the chair occupied by Mr. Weston, who had risen out of politeness and who joined the vicar, Mr. Elton, in leaning against a wall.

"Highbury will miss your mother," said Mrs. Weston, glancing at Mrs. Bates's empty chair, where she had spent most of the last few years of her life, knitting and nodding into naps. "She was a very good woman."

"She was, she was! She and my dear father, when they lived in the Vicarage, did so much for the poor. Everyone knew they could come for cheese, or for advice, or for bread, or for a cup of tea and a comforting word. Even in hard times she found a way to be generous, preparing baskets for the needy. A jar of broth, and depending on the season, apple tarts or homemade elderflower wine, dandelion salad or mushrooms she gathered from the forest herself. Mother could make even the smallest income go a long way; she was never stingy, but open-handed."

Mrs. Knightley thought that this description of the generosity of the prior inhabitants of the Vicarage would not gratify its current residents, the Eltons, who were also in the room and who both colored and frowned. To hide her amusement, so inappropriate for this occasion, Emma put her hand over her mouth but she could not resist glancing with mirthful eyes at Mrs. Weston, whose lips twitched. Mr. Weston, apparently sharing their understanding, coughed and put his empty cake plate down on a small table and then leaned back against the wall, while Mrs. Cole agreed with Miss Bates that Mrs. Bates, when she lived at the Vicarage, had enhanced its reputation for true Christian charity.

"No one ever said she did not," said Mrs. Elton with some asperity, while Mr. Elton looked down and fiddled with his shirt cuffs.

Miss Bates, as genuinely artless as she was loquacious, finally comprehended and tried to dispel this poor reflection on her callers. "Oh, Mrs. Elton, you don't – I didn't – I mean, times change and so how could anyone expect the Vicarage to be what it was thirty years ago? *You* have added so much elegance and refinement to Highbury. No other mistress of the Vicarage wore such lace, Mrs. Elton."

As Emma was not certain that these words would entirely do away with the Eltons' displeasure, for Mr. Elton continued to look uncomfortable and it was difficult to argue that Mrs. Elton's liberal purchases of fine lace were entirely in keeping with being liberal towards the poor, Emma decided it would be charitable to steer the conversation to safer waters. "You have certainly informed the Churchills, have you not, Miss Bates, of your mother's death?" asked Mrs. Knightley.

"Oh! Yes, we have. Or rather, Mr. Weston here was kind enough to take care of sending the message."

"Well, I have traveled to London many times myself and sent messages there even more frequently," said Mr. Weston, a man in his early fifties who was in business with his brothers in the city. "Taking care of the message was the least I could do. Frank and Jane certainly will come if they can, Miss Bates. You can be assured of that."

"It would be such a comfort! To see them here! And of course Jane must miss her grandmamma terribly. But they may be too busy," said Miss Bates.

"Nonsense! They will certainly come," Mr. Weston repeated. "That is why we have scheduled the funeral for the day after tomorrow; it will give them sufficient time to make the journey."

"I have confidence in my son-in-law, and you, Miss Bates, know how very attentive your niece is," said Mrs. Weston. "I agree with my husband: Frank and Jane will come to grieve with you."

Mr. and Mrs. Frank Churchill were a couple who both had their roots in Highbury, even though neither Frank Churchill nor Jane Fairfax Churchill had grown up in that placid village. Frank Weston Churchill was Mr. Weston's son, but had been raised from the age of two in distant Enscombe under the care of a wealthy uncle – his deceased mother's brother – and that uncle's wife. Upon reaching majority he had taken his rich uncle's name and was acknowledged to be that man's heir. He was, despite his removal from Highbury, the pride and joy of his father, Mr.

Weston, who had visited him once a year at least and had always returned home with reports so glowing that some doubted that a young man could be so tall, handsome, talented and good-natured. Mr. Frank Churchill, however, when he had finally made his appearance in Highbury for the first time not quite two years ago, had managed to live up to and even exceed the reputation that preceded him. All the women agreed that he was charming and even the men conceded he was good-looking.

Jane Fairfax Churchill was the granddaughter of Mrs. Bates through her deceased daughter, Jane Bates Fairfax, and a Lieutenant Fairfax. Due to the early demise of both her parents, Jane had spent the first part of her youth in Highbury, doted upon by her fond grandmother and cheerful aunt. For several years she was considered a tragic figure, rather like an exquisite flower in the forest, doomed to bloom then fade back into the earth unseen by all. Her superior beauty, talent and sensitive nature should have marked her out for greatness, but because of her nearest relatives' straightened means her prospects were extremely limited. Providence, however, seemed to change its mind and decided not to throw away its worthy creation. When Jane was still quite young she was taken in by friends of her father's, a Colonel Campbell and his wife, whose only living child was a girl about Jane's age. From that time the Campbells raised Jane with their daughter, teaching her, loving her, and sharing their lives with her. They were not, alas, able to provide her with a fortune – Colonel Campbell's thousands were not so many and had to be bestowed, he believed, on his daughter – but the education they provided to Jane Fairfax equipped her better for the challenges of the world.

Despite both being removed from what should have been their native home, Frank Churchill and Jane Fairfax had somehow met each other and had fallen in love and had become engaged – secretly engaged. Their romance was the favorite history of Highbury – two semi-orphans meeting and marrying despite obstacles – and perhaps the tale kept its luster all the more rosy because the principals no longer lived in Highbury. They were with Frank's rich uncle, the wealthy, genial Mr. Churchill. Other unions that had taken place about the same time had become ordinary in comparison. Mr. and Mrs. Weston – Mr. and Mrs. Elton – Mr. and Mrs. Robert Martin – even the marriage between Mr. Knightley and Miss Emma Woodhouse, representing the two most important families in the area – no matter how much happiness, or lack of it, those unions yielded to the parties involved, they could not match the entertainment provided by those speculating about Mr. Frank Churchill and his bride, Jane Fairfax. Since their marriage, the famous pair had only been once in Highbury, as the rich uncle, Mr. Churchill, was suffering from gout and needed his nephew and his wife to take care of him.

"I believe the Churchills should come," said Mrs. Elton. "It would be very wrong of them not to come. Don't you think so, Mr. E?"

"Yes, my dear," said Mr. Elton, who had picked up an old-fashioned gold locket from the top of the piano and seemed to be inspecting it with interest. "You are quite right."

"What are you doing, Mr. E?" asked Mrs. Elton, frowning at her husband with disapproval.

"That locket belonged to my mother," said Miss Bates. "It was the one valuable piece of jewelry that she owned and she wore It contains a lock of my father's hair – not that he had much when he died – and my sister's, too. Mother wore it every day and even when she was sick she insisted on having it with her."

"Ah! Very good, very good," said Mr. Elton but he put the locket back on the top of the pianoforte as hastily as if it were a hot lump of coal.

"Just looking at it makes me want to cry," said Miss Bates, blinking back tears as she surveyed her visitors, and moving over to the instrument. "It is mine now, but I have not yet made up my mind to wear it – it seems to still belong to my mother, do you understand? Or perhaps I should give it to Jane? That is why I put it on the pianoforte, because I always think of this as Jane's corner – she plays it so beautifully, everyone says so – but I am not sure about the locket. What do you think?"

"*You* should wear it, Miss Bates," Mrs. Weston assured her gently. "The locks of hair are from *your* father and *your* sister. You remember them best."

"Besides, Mrs. Churchill has plenty of other necklaces and jewels," added Emma.

"That is true," said Miss Bates, lifting up the locket. "To me – as it was to Mother – this locket is very precious, but the Mr. Churchills may not feel the same way. They may have other jewels that they prefer to see her wear."

"I'm sure Frank would appreciate the value of the locket," said Mr. Weston, who could not bear to hear any words that might even slightly disparage his son and his sensibilities, "but I am also sure that he would want you to keep it for yourself, Miss Bates."

"You are very generous, but it is too soon for you to be giving away your mother's things," said Mrs. Cole. "Mrs. Churchill will understand if you keep the locket."

Miss Bates, with all this encouragement from her friends, clutched the locket and took it back with her to her little chair and sat back down again.

"We have not seen Jane – I mean, Mrs. Churchill – for such a long time," Mrs. Elton spoke rather loudly, returning to the topic that interested her most. "I quite miss her." During Jane's last stay in Highbury – a visit of many months, which had only ended when her engagement to Mr. Frank

Churchill came to light – Mrs. Elton had made a fuss over Jane Fairfax, inviting her frequently over to the Vicarage for whist, music and meals. Among the young ladies of Highbury, Mrs. Elton had chosen Jane rather than Emma as her new, local confidante for many reasons, not the least being Emma's thinly veiled distaste for Mr. and Mrs. Elton. Mrs. Elton repeated herself: "It would be very rude of the Churchills not to come on this sad occasion."

"Indeed," echoed Mr. Elton. "Exactly so, my dear, but I am sure the Churchills will do what they can."

"Poor Jane will be so sad to learn of her grandmamma's passing," sighed Miss Bates, staring at the pianoforte. "How my mother loved to listen to her play the instrument."

Mrs. Weston complimented Miss Bates on the excellence of Jane's piano performance, while Emma's thoughts were divided between several inappropriate reactions to the mention of music. She experienced a bit of selfish alarm, because she realized that *she* had not practiced her instrument for more than a fortnight, and if Jane did come to Highbury, it would be impossible for anyone to listen to the two of them and consider her playing superior – a sad fact, but Jane was certainly the better musician and perhaps it was time to admit it. The other thought was just as unworthy – Mrs. Bates had been so deaf at the end, how could she possibly have enjoyed Jane's playing? But that thought was wrong and unchristian; even if she had not been able to appreciate the music, Mrs. Bates had certainly been happy to watch her granddaughter play.

Struggling to keep her unsuitable thoughts to herself, Emma missed part of the conversation, but when she attended again she discovered that everyone was continuing to agree that Jane Churchill's musical talent was superb, and that the Churchills should and would come to Highbury, both assertions equally pleasing to Miss Bates, the fond aunt. Just then the tiny apartment was invaded by more of Highbury's finest: the Perrys and the Otways and Mrs. Goddard. Miss Bates welcomed them with delight and gratitude, while Mrs. Knightley, Mrs. Weston, and Mr. and Mrs. Cole, in order to make room for the newcomers, decided to depart. Mr. Weston stayed behind, for Miss Bates wanted to consult with him about some pecuniary matters; given their family connection he often assisted her with advice and letter-writing. The Eltons also remained with Miss Bates, as Mr. Elton was the current vicar, and needed to settle certain details with Miss Bates regarding her mother's funeral.

Emma, feeling she had done her duty, descended the dark and narrow staircase, and then walked out into the sunlight.

2 STROLLING THROUGH HIGHBURY

It was a lovely day in early autumn, the air fresh and the sun warm and bright after the cramped and crowded apartment. The last few days had been free of rain, which was convenient for those checking their ricks of hay and getting in the harvest on the surrounding farms. The clemency of the recent weather meant the roads and paths were dry, which was also convenient for the shoes of gentlewomen walking from Highbury to their homes a little distance from the village. Mrs. Knightley and Mrs. Weston parted from the Coles, whose house was in a different direction, and then walked together.

Emma Woodhouse Knightley was happy to have a few moments alone with her friend Mrs. Weston. Mrs. Weston was the second wife of Mr. Weston, and hence the stepmother of Mr. Frank Churchill, the relationships in Highbury being as complicated as the dynasties of some of Europe's royal houses. Before marrying Mr. Weston, which joyful event had occurred about two years ago, Mrs. Weston had been Miss Anne Taylor and had resided with Emma at Hartfield as Emma's governess. Besides her husband, Mr. Knightley, there was no other person in the kingdom to whom Emma could speak her heart with such lack of reserve as she could with Mrs. Weston, who in addition to being her governess, had been her second mother and her dearest companion.

"Do *you* think the Churchills will come?" Emma asked.

"I think they will. They are not far, you know, having recently arrived in London from Yorkshire, and the season and the roads are good for traveling. Besides, ever since Mrs. Churchill's death they have been much more flexible."

"But are you certain? Have you heard anything?"

"No, but it is the right thing to do, to show Miss Bates attention on such an occasion. She must be feeling very melancholy."

7

"If you say so," said Emma, but a quirk of her lips indicated that the woman they had just called upon showed no symptoms of sinking into melancholia.

"Of course, all the company she is receiving right now is cheering her up," said Mrs. Weston, unable to stop herself from making this slight correction to her former pupil. "That was the point of our visit, Emma."

"You are absolutely right, Mrs. Weston," Emma acknowledged, and thought of her own father, beloved to her and not in the best of health. She might very well be the next person in Highbury to receive these condolatory visits. "What do you suppose Miss Bates will do, now that her mother is gone? She is so accustomed to having someone to care for."

"That is a good question, Emma, but Miss Bates will surely find a way to keep busy. Perhaps the Churchills will assist in that matter."

"The Eltons are most eager that the Churchills should come to Highbury just now – they are more eager even than you and Mr. Weston," Emma observed. "I mean no reflection on you and Mr. Weston, but the Eltons show unsurpassed zeal."

"The minister and his wife must know how much Miss Bates would welcome a visit from Jane right now."

"And the Churchills will certainly give a larger donation to the church on the occasion of Mrs. Bates's funeral than Miss Bates would on her own," added Emma.

Mrs. Weston laughed but scolded Emma anyway. "For shame, Emma! You are finding levity on a serious occasion."

"Forgive me, my dear friend. You know that I have an unserious side – there is a part of me that needs to laugh, and after a condolence visit such as this, my mirth needs to be released and exercised."

"I understand, dear Emma, and your wit has given me great enjoyment over the years. But take care – not everyone would appreciate it."

"And my levity does no credit to you, either, who raised me." They were fast approaching Hartfield, the large house and its well-manicured grounds just beyond the great iron sweep-gate. Emma waved towards the house, where Mrs. Weston had resided so many years as well. "Remember that when I am home right now, there is no laughter. My father feels Mrs. Bates's death far more keenly than any of the rest of us."

"Ah, Emma, I know. Mr. Woodhouse remembers Mrs. Bates from his own young days, and it must be so sad to think of one of his oldest friends gone. Give my best to him, my dear, and to Mr. Knightley, and kiss your baby for me."

Emma likewise gave her friend best wishes, and walked through the sweep gate towards her house. How lovely it was to enter her own home, so spacious and orderly and comfortable and full of family. It reminded her to think with compassion of Miss Bates, whose apartment was so small and who had just lost her mother – the woman she had lived with her entire life.

In the foyer, her mood once again suitably serious, Emma removed her hat and coat, learned from a servant that the baby was taking a nap, and prepared herself to go speak to her father in the parlor.

Mr. Woodhouse was anxious to learn about her visit in Highbury. "How was everyone, my dear? My dear old friend Miss Bates?"

"She is doing very well, Papa. Many people were calling on her."

The old man sighed. "I should have gone to see her myself. But that staircase – I never liked that staircase. Still, on such an occasion I should have made the effort."

"No, Papa, that was not necessary. The staircase is as steep and narrow as you remember and besides, the apartment was very crowded. You would have made yourself ill. I assure you that Miss Bates understands quite well that you are not up to it, and she thanked me for your kind note. She was very grateful for your note, Papa."

"*You* wrote it, my dear," remarked Mr. Woodhouse, with more self-awareness than usual, possibly brought on by the contemplation of the passing of one of his contemporaries.

"But it was your thought, Papa. Miss Bates, more than anyone, appreciates the kindness of your thoughts. I only expressed them for you."

"I am not up to anything, my dear Emma. It will be my turn next."

Even though Emma had harbored the same notion just a few minutes earlier, she was quick to contradict her father. "No, Papa, don't say any such thing!"

"At least Mrs. Bates went in her sleep, says my friend Mr. Perry," mused Mr. Woodhouse. Mr. Perry was the local apothecary and a frequent visitor to Mr. Woodhouse at Hartfield. "Ah, my dear, it will be my turn next."

Emma sought a way to rouse him out of his unhappy reflections, and reminded him that he had walked around the garden earlier that day, and how well he had mentioned feeling just a few days ago. These cheerful thoughts reduced the frequency and duration of his sighs. Then Emma re-read to him a letter that had come the day before from his eldest daughter, Isabella, who lived in London, and they had a discussion about how well her husband, Mr. John Knightley – the younger brother of Emma's own husband – how well Mr. John Knightley, a lawyer, was doing in his profession. These reminders of his eldest daughter stopped Mr. Woodhouse from sighing. Finally the nursemaid told Emma that the baby was awake, and when little George was brought and carefully placed in his grandfather's lap, Mr. Woodhouse actually smiled.

As dusk was falling, they heard Mr. Knightley entering through Hartfield's front door. He arrived, full of life and news about his farm and the harvest. Even Mr. Woodhouse could not resist his son-in-law's good humor as Mr. Knightley talked about the bushels of apples, the yipping dogs and the antics of one of Farmer Gilbert's young bulls. A large bull calf had crashed its way through the hedgerows, and had left the Gilbert farm for Donwell Abbey, Mr. Knightley's estate.

"An animal of both good breeding and taste!" Emma exclaimed.

"Just so," said Mr. Knightley.

Her husband's smile let her know that he comprehended her compliment to Donwell Abbey. How lovely it was to be married to a man who not only understood her quick wit but who appreciated it! But both Mr. and Mrs. Knightley realized that the multiple meanings to Emma's remark could not be understood by Mr. Woodhouse, so they deferred their pleasantries until later.

"What did the animal do?" asked the old gentleman.

Mr. Knightley, dancing his baby on his knee, explained that the bull calf had made its way into Mr. Knightley's kitchen garden, and had contentedly and determinedly grazed on turnip leaves while Mrs. Hodges, Mr. Knightley's cook, had alternated between useless terror and impotent fury. The rest of them had tried to chase it off with dogs, sticks and shouts, but the animal refused to budge. Then one of Gilbert's temporary workers, a gypsy fellow named Draper hired for the duration of the harvest, had an idea. Without consulting anyone, he returned to Gilbert's farm and came back with a cow. Draper then suggested introducing the cow into the garden, and said that they could use her to tempt the bull to leave. This solution did not please Mrs. Hodges, who did not want another bovine trampling her turnips, and even Mr. Knightley admitted that he had had his doubts.

But Gilbert said they should follow Draper's advice. "He's clever with animals," said the other farmer.

Mr. Knightley finally consented, and while Mrs. Hodges frowned from her place near the door, the farmer's worker led the cow into the turnips. The young bull noticed the cow, greeted it with affection – and then when Draper led the cow out of the kitchen garden, the young bull followed at last.

"Well, I never!" said Mrs. Hodges, descending from her position of safety, and approaching Mr. Knightley, Mr. Gilbert and William Larkins, who worked for Mr. Knightley. From the edge of the garden they watched Draper leading the animals away.

"Draper's a magician," said Mr. Gilbert, some pride in his voice.

"Gypsy magic, is it?" asked William Larkins, who was frustrated by his failure to get the bull calf to leave the Donwell garden. The gypsies who came through and worked on some of the farms during the busy seasons were resented by some of the Highbury and Donwell yeomen.

"Nothing like that," said Mr. Gilbert placidly, who was aware of the local prejudice but nevertheless hired Draper and the others in his clan, for he was pleased with their work. "That was the bull's mother."

Gilbert then apologized to Mr. Knightley for the time and trouble that his animal had taken, and especially to Mrs. Hodges for having given her such a fright. He promised to send over a basket of his garden's best parsnips, to make up for the damage that his bull calf had caused – and later, when the animal was killed, several excellent steaks.

The prospect of good beef softened the crusty Hodges, although she could not completely admit it, and she only said pointedly that she *hoped* there would be someone at Donwell Abbey to eat it. She then went back inside. The turnips were once more at peace, and everyone returned to their tasks.

Emma was perceptive enough to discern Mrs. Hodges's displeasure at her master's not being around to eat her dinners. She glanced at Mr. Knightley, who shrugged in understanding. Their marriage had inconvenienced those at Donwell Abbey, but while her father lived, she was needed at Hartfield.

Mr. Woodhouse was concerned about the security of the grounds. "Are you taking steps to make sure it does not happen again?" he asked. "How did the animal get into the estate in the first place?"

Mr. Knightley explained that he could not control Gilbert's herd, but he had given William Larkins the task of repairing the gate. Somehow the latch had broken or else the animal would never have gotten in.

They learned then that dinner was ready. Emma and her father consumed their usual portions, but Mr. Knightley, hungry after his long day working his farm, had several helpings of goose and fried pork. Emma watching him, relaxed. Mrs. Hodges might not want to believe it, but Mr. Knightley, despite living at Hartfield, was eating well.

3 EXCURSIONS OF A LIVELY MIND

Emma had once believed that being married to Mr. Knightley would steady her. But a lively mind, although it may respect and admire steadiness, although it may give that virtue all its due, does not always enjoy being in that state. Nearly a year of marriage and the birth of their son a few months before had given her ample opportunity to become more sober – yet Emma had discovered that she actually preferred to let her imagination run free, and that attempting to restrict her thoughts was annoying.

"Your father used to scold me for meddling," Emma told her child, who had decided to stay awake that night, even though his grandfather and most of the servants were asleep in their beds. Baby George's good humor, though, made his wakefulness a pleasure instead of a penance, especially for the father who had been gone all day tending his farm in the next parish, and Emma talked to the baby as he lay on her lap and pulled her finger. "He was right; I did meddle, and poorly too as I guessed wrong in several instances. But I still think there is value in observing people and trying to understand what they are about, Baby George."

Mr. Knightley, who was changing into his nightclothes, overheard everything that was nominally being addressed to his son, but which both parents knew was really meant for him. "My dear wife, what are you planning?"

"You will not reproach me for thinking and wondering, will you?" Emma asked archly.

"As long as you confine yourself to thinking and wondering, and do not actually interfere in others' lives, I have no objection; indeed, I encourage it, " said Mr. Knightley tolerantly, who as he was sixteen years older than his wife, and knew how people did and did not change, had never expected that their marriage would reform his wife's character.

"What are you thinking and wondering, then?" he asked, settling in a comfortable chair and reaching for his son. "I am interested to listen to it."

Emma was happy to hear this and she told him of some of what had happened when she had made her condolence call to Miss Bates. Then she brought up the point that was intriguing her. "Why are the Eltons so eager for the Churchills to come to Highbury for the funeral of old Mrs. Bates?"

"Ah, your favorite enemies, the Eltons! Baby George, I hope you will not inherit your mother's dislikes, and will be friends with young Philip Elton," Mr. Knightley advised his son, who gurgled in response.

The Eltons also had an infant son, a few months older than the Knightleys' child.

"Well, it is much more pleasant to think bad thoughts about people we don't like, rather than bad thoughts about those we do."

"That is absolutely true, but not terribly Christian," Mr. Knightley said. "The subject might make a good sermon for Elton."

"You will not suggest it to him, I hope!" Emma responded in horror. Mr. Elton's sermons had improved since he started reading the works by others rather than trying to preach one of his own, for his own essays were too full of poetry and fine flourishes for the prosaic taste of Highbury. He still occasionally inflicted an original on his poor parish.

"So Mrs. Elton has had at least one good influence on Mr. Elton," Mr. Knightley said, making faces at his son. "What dark secrets do you ascribe to them? Why can't they simply wish for Miss Bates to be comforted by her nearest relatives?"

"My notion – laugh at it if you will – is that the Eltons want the Churchills to come down in time for the funeral, not just to comfort their dear friend Miss Bates, but because the Churchills would very likely make a large donation to the Vicarage on the occasion. There!" she added smilingly, as she rearranged her combs and brushes on her table. "I think them avaricious, that is all."

Mr. Knightley scratched his chin. "You may be correct, Emma."

Emma was delighted. "Really? *You* think *I* may be correct?"

"Well, the returns on Mrs. Elton's thousands may not be as high as they were two years ago."

"And we all know that Mr. Suckling's business has suffered due to complications arising from the slave trade," said Emma. Mr. Suckling was the wealthy brother-in-law of Mrs. Elton. Emma had never actually met the man; the Sucklings had been promising a visit to Highbury for several years, ever since the Eltons married, but somehow the visit was always postponed. Still, Mrs. Elton spoke so frequently about her wealthy brother-in-law and his estate, Maple Grove, that Emma could not escape knowing many details, as did the rest of Highbury.

Mr. Knightley frowned at this mention of the slave trade, which he found abhorrent, but with the baby on his lap he did not go into his usual tirade about the despicable practices in the Americas. Instead he confined himself to a grunt, which was open to many interpretations, then reached for a cloth from Emma, for the child was drooling.

"And Mrs. Elton simply must have the finest lace for her gowns, for all that she likes them simply made," Emma continued hastily, regretting having mentioned the slave trade, which she too found dreadful, but also too distant to be relevant to their lives.

"Yet I cannot believe that a donation made on the occasion of a funeral would be so significant as to make a material difference to the Eltons' income."

"Perhaps they will try again to improve the church," said Emma. As Emma's father was the richest man in Highbury, the Eltons had already appealed to Mr. Woodhouse for funds to support this ambition. Mr. Woodhouse was a generous man, and had assisted the families in the region his entire life, but when Emma studied the petition, she could not countenance the expense proposed by the Eltons. It was sizable and seemed to be designed more to serve the splendor of the parson than the comfort of the parish. Emma's conclusions had been supported by Mr. Knightley, the Coles, and even the affable Mr. Weston, and so had been dropped, although with many loud regrets about the short-sightedness of Highbury parishioners. But the Churchills, even wealthier than the Woodhouses, could be a new source for this scheme. "They could name it after Mrs. Bates. As Mrs. Bates's husband was a vicar, the Eltons could get Miss Bates — and through her, Mrs. Churchill — to support it."

"That is a possibility, and not totally unsuitable. But if the scheme pleases the Eltons and the Churchills do not mind, what business is it of ours?"

"None at all," Emma was forced to admit.

"When is the funeral?" asked Mr. Knightley.

Emma informed him that it would take place the day after next, in the morning, which would give the Churchills enough time to come down from London if they were so inclined.

"I saw Weston on my way back from Donwell," said Mr. Knightley. "He told me that Mr. and Mrs. Frank Churchill are expected to arrive in their carriage late tomorrow."

"He is sure they will come?" Emma asked. "Or does he only hope it?"

They both knew Mr. Weston to be among the most optimistic of men, and although it made him a cheerful and pleasant acquaintance, it meant that sometimes his assumptions about the future were not the most reliable.

"He assures me that they have received a letter to that effect," Mr. Knightley reported. "Depend on it if you will."

"Although I should like to see the Churchills, their visit matters far less to me than it will to Miss Bates. And, of course, to the Eltons." She wondered if there were any way to ascertain the condition of the finances at the Vicarage.

"Mrs. Bates's funeral is two days from now," Mr. Knightley said, tickling his baby's chin. "If you are at liberty tomorrow, you could use the time to visit your friend Harriet Martin."

"And why do you recommend that I do that?" Emma asked.

Harriet Smith Martin had been a serious point of contention between them before their own marriage. Harriet was the source of Emma's deepest self-recriminations, for she had persuaded her young, pretty and gullible friend not to marry Robert Martin when he first proposed, but had convinced Harriet that Mr. Elton, who was then single, admired Harriet. When that scheme burst – and in the most embarrassing manner possible, as Mr. Elton had proved himself devoted to Emma instead, or at least to the thirty thousand pounds that came with her – Emma had discovered how little insight she had into the human heart and how inept she was at matchmaking.

At the time, Harriet's refusal of Robert Martin had infuriated Mr. Knightley. Mr. Knightley was fond of young Robert Martin, his tenant at the Abbey-Mill Farm and had encouraged the yeoman farmer in his courtship of Harriet Smith. Mr. Knightley had rightly blamed Emma, and not Harriet for the refusal.

She was incorrigible, Emma thought, for even her failure to understand Mr. Elton's intentions had not stopped her matchmaking. Without actively meddling, Emma had next hoped for a marriage between Mr. Frank Churchill and Harriet, while Harriet herself – proving that she had the best taste in gentlemen, even if she was not the wisest in the selection of her female companions – Harriet decided that Mr. Knightley himself was the man superior to everyone, and lost her heart to him. Emma could comfort herself with the thought that in the latter part of that year of blundering romances she had not truly behaved in such a way as to merit being described as interfering. She had never explicitly encouraged Harriet Martin to think of Mr. Knightley or even of Mr. Frank Churchill; in fact, she had counseled Harriet against aiming so high. Perhaps her warnings could have been stronger and more emphatically worded, but Emma had little to truly upbraid herself about – at least in that matter.

But, all's well that ends well, and despite her scheming and plotting, her imagining and hoping, a good fairy had somehow managed to match all the right husbands with the right wives, in an arrangement so perfect that it was a wonder that no one had perceived the pairings beforehand. Mr. Elton, refused by Emma Woodhouse and disgusted at the notion of allying himself with Harriet Smith – who was young and pretty but silly and poor and moreover the natural daughter of an unknown tradesman – Mr. Elton had gone to Bath where he found the eminently suitable, ten-thousand-pound-dowered Augusta Hawkins. Mr. Knightley had proposed to Emma, while his yeoman farming tenant Robert Martin had renewed his suit to Harriet Smith.

The great surprise, however, was the secret engagement between Jane Fairfax and Mr. Frank Churchill. That matter still embarrassed Emma, on several accounts. She had been suspicious of Jane Fairfax's visit of many months to Highbury, which Jane had arranged under pretexts that sounded weak to Emma. Jane's real reason for staying in Highbury was to make it easier for her fiancé, Mr. Frank Churchill, to visit her whenever he went there to see his natural father. (Their Highbury relatives – especially Mr. and Mrs. Weston – were for those months honored with more attention from the secretly engaged pair than they had ever known before.) Emma, however, despite her pride in her ability to perceive budding romances, never suspected the alliance between Jane and Frank. Some credit must go to the pair, who were of course trying to keep their secret betrothal secret, but Emma's complete and utter blindness in the matter wounded her vanity. Furthermore, Emma had voiced her suspicions about Jane in such a way that reached Jane and angered that young woman.

So Emma had mixed feelings about the prospect of seeing the Churchills again, for although they were significant additions to Highbury society, which generally had so little variation, unpleasant memories and self-recriminations would intrude. On the other hand, the funeral would be a sad, formal occasion, and if she behaved with discreet correctness she would not embarrass herself or anyone else.

Mr. Knightley's thoughts had not strayed so far; he was still occupied by the condition of Harriet Smith Martin. Mr. Knightley jiggled his baby on his lap, and then addressed his wife. "She will be happy to tell you all the details, but her husband let me know she is expecting again."

"So soon!" Emma exclaimed, her mind returning to the Martins and especially to Harriet. Harriet, who always had difficulty making any decision, from whether she wanted blue ribbon or yellow to which man she loved, had been that way as a mother. As if her body could not decide whether she should produce a boy or a girl, she had given birth to twins, one of each, only a few months before. "She must be exhausted."

"Robert Martin says she is," Mr. Knightley confirmed. "And with his mother and sister away, the household is more than she can manage."

"That does not surprise me," said Emma. "Very well, tomorrow I will visit Harriet Martin." The baby slumbered at last, and so she took him from his father and carried him to his crib in the room down the hall.

When she returned, she confirmed to Mr. Knightley's query that their son was still asleep, and then went back to speculating about the Eltons, their finances and their interest in the Churchills.

"Perhaps if I see them together, I will discern more," she concluded, climbing into bed beside him.

Mr. Knightley, fatigued from his long day, yawned. "Observe all you like, my dear Emma. I only request that you do and say nothing indiscreet."

Emma sighed. "Well, I will only watch. I won't interfere. Besides, if you think we are making unpleasant conjectures about the Eltons, only consider what they are thinking and wondering about us! Why do we have neighbors, if we can't think and wonder about them?"

He laughed, pulled her close, and went to sleep.

4 MRS. WESTON'S MORNING CALL

The next morning they rose as usual. Mr. Woodhouse was less weighed upon by the death of Mrs. Bates and more concerned with a slight soreness in the back of the throat that troubled him when he woke; Emma immediately wrote a note to Mr. Perry, Highbury's apothecary, asking if he could stop by later that day. Then they had a serious discussion with her father about whether he should take his usual walk in the Hartfield shrubbery.

"I don't know if I should go out," said Mr. Woodhouse. "I should protect my throat from chill air."

"But sir, the sun is up and the air is warm," replied Mr. Knightley. "There is no chill in the air. Besides, you said yourself that your throat was feeling better since you drank a cup of tea."

"I want my throat to stay better," said Mr. Woodhouse, staring dubiously out the window at the shrubbery in the golden morning light.

"Papa, why not wear your hat and your scarf?" suggested Emma. "That will prevent any chill."

Mr. Woodhouse considered his daughter's suggestion. "I suppose I could wear my scarf. That is a good idea, Emma. You are always so clever!"

"Sir, you know you always feel better after you take your morning walk," Mr. Knightley encouraged him. "It invigorates you, sir."

Emboldened by the use of the word "invigorates" to describe him, Mr. Woodhouse accepted his scarf from his daughter and went out the door for his morning constitutional.

"You are always so patient with him," Emma remarked to Mr. Knightley.

"And why should I not be?" said her husband.

"Not all husbands would be so understanding," Emma said. "We have variations of the same conversation with him every morning."

"And you deal with far more of it than I, with unfailing good-humor. I sometimes worry, Emma, that your life is too dull for a woman of your wit. But quick, while your father is taking his walk, let us discuss today."

They hastily settled what they would do that day. Frequently they called on the Westons – Mr. Woodhouse included – or the Westons called on them. Shortly after the birth of little Anna Weston, Mr. Woodhouse had been persuaded to make morning visits to the Westons. The visits were not long, for Mr. Woodhouse tired easily, but they had been regular.

However, in the last few months, the routine had altered. Little Anna Weston was now more than a year old, while the Knightleys had their own infant, and so it was easier for the Westons to travel the half mile from Randalls to Hartfield, which at least Mrs. Weston usually did, bringing her daughter. Mr. Weston was a little less regular, as he frequently called away by business, but no one could fault his lack of attention.

"Do you think the Westons will come today, or will the arrival of the Churchills prevent it?" asked Emma, as the wet-nurse arrived with Baby George and handed him to Emma.

"They are not expected until late in the day, so I don't see why Mrs. Weston would not come. She knows how much your father likes to see Anna."

Just as they were having this discussion, a note arrived from Randalls, promising a visit from Mrs. Weston later that morning with her child; Mr. Weston would not be coming. Mrs. Weston, so long an inmate at Hartfield, knew how important the routine of her visit was to Mr. Woodhouse's health and spirits, and she also knew how much Hartfield would appreciate the certainty supplied by her note.

"And you are going to Donwell?"

"The harvest needs me," Mr. Knightley said. "I also want to check on the cider press."

Donwell Abbey was Mr. Knightley's estate, a few miles away from Hartfield, in the next parish. Despite having an estate of his own, Mr. Knightley, in order to be able to live with his wife, had moved in with Emma and her elderly father. But Mr. Knightley, having a good deal of energy and a desire to be in his own home – and although he was always very patient with Mr. Woodhouse, the lack of energy in his father-in-law had to be a trial – was constantly going back and forth. Emma, well aware that the sacrifice of independence was difficult for her husband, encouraged Mr. Knightley to visit his own estate as often as he could.

"Of course, Mr. Knightley," Emma said. "If you like, I can pick you up later in the carriage."

"You can?" he asked, frowning a little at this offer, for he was rather proud and did not like riding in his father-in-law's carriage, even though he conceded that James the coachman was bored and that the Woodhouse horses needed exercise. He usually refused, explaining that he did not want to inconvenience Mrs. Knightley or Mr. Woodhouse, in case they needed the carriage while he was gone. "Where are you going?" he asked, and then answered his own question: "To see Harriet, of course."

"Yes, after Mrs. Weston leaves, I will go and see how Harriet is faring. But first I will stop at Ford's and buy her some baby things."

"That is a generous and considerate idea, Emma."

"Emma is always generous and considerate," said Mr. Woodhouse, who had finished his walk and was back inside, pleased with himself for making the effort.

"Yes, sir, she is," Mr. Knightley agreed, and he had his own reasons for agreement, for some of Emma's fortune had been used to patch up the roof of a barn at Donwell Abbey and to install a few new windows. This was also difficult for Mr. Knightley, who preferred not to be indebted to his wife, but Emma had gently reasoned with him that the windows and the barn would later be part of *their* home and certainly belong to their children. Still, he refused to let her buy another pair of horses, and so she had to resort to stratagems to get him to agree to use the ones belonging to the Woodhouses.

"Make sure you take your coat, my dear," said Emma, "it looks as if it may rain."

"Rain?" asked Mr. Woodhouse, alarmed. "Mr. Knightley, you should not go out if it looks as if it will rain."

Mr. Knightley frowned at Emma for having used this particular trick, because now Mr. Woodhouse now worried about his son-in-law possibly getting wet. "Emma knows very well that it does not look like rain. Did you see any clouds in the sky, sir?"

"Don't worry, Papa, it is only a joke. Mr. Knightley will not get rained on. I am only trying to persuade him to let me fetch him in the carriage later. It was only a ruse, and I am sorry for it."

"You should let Emma fetch you in the carriage, Mr. Knightley," said Mr. Woodhouse. "Why should you walk such a great distance when you don't need to?"

Emma had won the point – she would be able to continue to Donwell Abbey to pick up her husband, but Mr. Knightley's expression showed that he was displeased by the manipulation.

"That was not fair," he said.

"What was not fair?" she asked.

"You know what I mean," he said, his voice low.

"Of course, I am a terrible wife because I want to keep you from overtiring yourself," said Emma. "Some men would not be ashamed to be fetched in their wives' carriages."

"I am not some men," he retorted.

"No, certainly not! You prefer to walk in the rough and to ruin your shoes instead of to ride in comfort. Let me remind you that *you* told me yesterday that I should visit Harriet today, so my taking out the carriage today is simply evidence of my good-natured obedience. And since I will be out in the carriage, at the Martins, not far from Donwell, it would be foolish of me not to have James take the horses just a little further. They will be glad for the exercise and you should be glad for the rest, after working hard all day on your cider press or your ricks of hay or whatever project you and William Larkins are addressing today."

Her gentle tirade drew out a smile, as she had intended. "Nonsensical girl!" he exclaimed, and bent down to kiss her cheek. "You are welcome to take a look at my current projects, as you call them."

"And if you think I am concerned that you married me for my money, you can rest assured that you have long since convinced me that that was not the case."

This elicited another smile, followed by a thoughtful look, and Emma was certain that she had somehow gotten near the truth.

They agreed that she would leave after Mrs. Weston's visit, spend some time at Harriet's and then continue on to Donwell in mid-afternoon, so that they could be home before dark. Mr. Woodhouse approved of this plan as well, then Mr. Knightley kissed his baby and his wife, shook hands with his father-in-law, then set off at a brisk pace for his estate.

Emma spent the next hour playing with her baby and encouraging her father to consume some gruel. Then Mrs. Weston arrived with her little daughter for their morning visit.

The first quarter hour was spent as it was always spent: Mrs. Weston asking Mr. Woodhouse about his health, hearing about the sore throat that he had had upon waking – but how much better he felt after his little walk. "Invigorated," said the gentle old man, repeating the word given him by his son-in-law. Mr. Woodhouse then inquired, with particular minuteness, about the health of all the Westons, complimenting Mrs. Weston and the little girl on their rosy cheeks.

"The air of Randalls certainly agrees with you," said Mr. Woodhouse. "I think you would still do better at Hartfield, but if you cannot live here, then Randalls seems to suit."

"I assure you, Mr. Woodhouse, we are all very well."

Emma in the meantime had taken out a few toys for little Anna. They had a nursery full of toys, saved for the visits of her sister Isabella and her children from London, and Emma always had one or two at hand for

Anna's visits. Baby George, still too small to do more than wave his tiny fists, stared enviously at little Anna Weston – to him she was certainly big Anna Weston – as she made her unsteady way to a wax doll which had its own little chair, at a safe distance from both the fireplace and sunbeams.

After Mr. Woodhouse and Mrs. Weston had made their usual exchanges – and Mrs. Weston had more patience in this matter than many others – and the children were amusing one another – Mrs. Weston and Mrs. Emma Knightley could exchange some words about the little items that mattered most to them.

Of chief interest was the new pregnancy of Harriet Martin; Mrs. Weston, who had started motherhood rather late in life, could only shake her head and say, "Oh, dear!" and hope that the much younger Harriet was not too fatigued. Emma then asked if it was true that the Churchills were coming to attend the funeral of Mrs. Bates?

"We received a note assuring us that that is their intention," Mrs. Weston replied.

"Very correct of them," said Mr. Woodhouse, catching this part of the conversation, and then shaking his head and sighing, "Poor Mrs. Bates," and sinking back into melancholy reverie.

"And yet?" Emma probed, for she had known Mrs. Weston too long not to catch every change in tone. "Do you doubt that they will come?"

"I have no reason to doubt them," Mrs. Weston said with a smile, which Emma knew to mean that she did doubt them, even if she had no reason. "They are in London these days, not so far from here, and although Mr. Churchill's health is not good, there is no reason to think that his situation is so severe as to prevent them from coming to Highbury for a few days. Miss Bates would certainly welcome such a visit – as would Mr. Weston and myself."

"And yet?" Emma pressed again, knowing that her friend was reluctant to share private details that might be troubling her, and yet believing, too, that Mrs. Weston would feel better once she confided in someone.

"Something makes me uneasy. Mr. Weston makes light of it – of course – but I wonder if Jane and Frank are entirely happy with each other. Or perhaps Mr. Churchill is being difficult. I have not seen them for some time, so I confess I do not know. Although Frank writes regularly, his letters are not as long nor as revealing as they were earlier, but I sense that Jane is unhappy about something."

"Perhaps Mrs. Churchill is unwell?" asked Emma, for she had heard rumors of a miscarriage several months ago.

"Possibly," said Mrs. Weston.

"Mr. Weston has seen them in London, but I have not, and so I am dependent on Mr. Weston's observations. He tells me everything is fine, but he has always been hopeful."

"You will have a chance to observe them yourself, beginning today," Emma assured her. "Then you can advise them and comfort them, if necessary, or set your kind heart at rest."

"True," said Mrs. Weston. "I may be borrowing trouble unnecessarily. And now, I must make sure their room is ready. Come, Anna!" and she held out her hand to her little girl. "We have to go prepare the house for your brother."

Mrs. Weston and her daughter said goodbye to Mr. Woodhouse and to Baby George – the latter, so fascinated by Anna Weston, wailed for a full two minutes after their departure, before being distracted by the sight of a large bird that flew outside the window – but Mr. Woodhouse was content. He wondered a little about Mr. Churchill's illness, and then dozed off in his chair.

Emma, humming to her baby, was also content, for her mind had plenty to nourish it. Harriet's pregnancy – the Eltons' finances – and now the Frank Churchills' marriage. Mr. Knightley might be concerned that her life was too trivial and too dull, and certainly it might appear so to others, but for Emma, so accustomed to have to amuse herself with so little, these morsels were rich meals for her imagination.

5 HARRIET MARTIN IS TERRIFIED

Mr. Perry arrived shortly before midday, occupying Mr. Woodhouse with attentive solicitude and trivial gossip. Emma made sure that everyone – her baby and her father – were in good hands, and told James to take out the carriage and to prepare to drive, first to Ford's, second to Abbey-Mill Farm, where the Martins lived, and last to Donwell Abbey.

"Fine day for a drive, Ma'am," said the coachman James, who, despite Mr. Woodhouse's worries and Mr. Knightley's pride, was pleased to be taking himself and the horses out for exercise. He opened the carriage door and helped her step inside.

Emma agreed that it was, indeed, a fine day for a drive and she even let down the window to enjoy the sunshine. At Ford's she placed an order for linens and bibs to be sent to the Martins, as well as a few blue ribbons for Harriet to wear in her hair. Then, realizing that Harriet might not be in a position to play the part of the hostess with ease, she crossed the street to the bakery. There she purchased a loaf of bread and some fresh tarts and a jar of honey. As she was leaving the baker's she encountered Mrs. Elton, coming out of the door that led to the Bates apartment.

Only a few feet away from each other, the meeting could not be avoided, and etiquette obliged them to greet each other. Mrs. Elton asked, with rather abrupt inquisitiveness, what Mrs. Knightley was doing there. "Buying bread, I see. Don't you have servants who do that? Or is there something wrong with the Hartfield ovens?"

"Yes, but I happened to be here. I was just over at Ford's."

"Buying the blue silk, I take it? Mrs. Ford tells me they just received a new shipment and that it is absolutely exquisite."

"I did not look at the blue silk," Emma said. Realizing she would never escape from Mrs. Elton without explaining what she had been doing, she added, "I was preparing an order of baby linens for Harriet Martin."

"Ah, yes! Your intimate friend, Harriet Martin," said Mrs. Elton, with a sneer. Shortly after her arrival in Highbury, Mrs. Elton had developed a scornful attitude towards poor Harriet, and had never overcome it.

Emma heard the disdain in Mrs. Elton's voice, but instead of responding to it she changed the subject by asking Mrs. Elton if she had called again on Miss Bates. Mrs. Elton acknowledged that she had. "As the vicar's wife I feel it is my duty as a Christian to condole with those grieving in the parish as much as I can."

"Most excellent of you," said Emma, with as much composure as she could muster, for she thought Mrs. Elton would be well-served to apply Christian virtues in other areas.

"Of course there is only so much that *I* can do. Miss Bates can really only be comforted by her niece. But I believe that the Churchills are coming to Highbury, are they not?"

Emma would have loved to keep Mrs. Elton in suspense over this, but there was no point in trying to keep such a piece of information secret in Highbury. "That is what Mrs. Weston told me this morning," Emma said.

"And what Miss Bates told me just now," Mrs. Elton said. "Well! We will see if they keep their word. Very important to keep their word. Good day, Mrs. Knightley."

Emma was just as relieved as Mrs. Elton to finish their conversation, and after wishing Mrs. Elton a pleasant day, returned to her carriage. She was grateful, too, that the Vicarage was in a different direction from Donwell Abbey or she would have felt obliged to offer Mrs. Elton a ride - even though the day was as pleasant for walking as any the season in Surrey could offer.

The horses pulled her carriage along the hedgerow-lined lane, past fields where a boy and a pair of dogs were herding a flock of sheep from one field to another, and an orchard where men and youths were picking apples. But Emma barely noticed these pastoral sights, instead becoming more convinced than ever that something was amiss with the Eltons' finances. She wondered how she could acquire confirmation – perhaps an inquiry into their accounts at Ford's – a look into the church books – gossip from their servants, but most servants in Highbury were fiercely loyal in such matters. These thoughts occupied Emma's mind until the carriage reached the Abbey-Mill Farm. She dismissed one scheme and then another; Mr. Knightley would not approve of her being too obviously curious!

James brought the carriage to a halt, and then assisted his mistress to descend, helping her with the basket of bread and honey. Then Emma went through the yard and knocked. There was no answer, but she heard a child crying inside, which meant that someone was home – so Emma waited on the step. Harriet could be busy; Harriet could easily be overwhelmed. Emma knocked again; again there was no answer; only the sound of the crying child – or, listening hard, and given that Harriet had twins, perhaps *two* crying children.

Emma was loath to enter uninvited, but she recalled that Mrs. Martin, Harriet's mother-in-law, was away with Miss Elizabeth Martin, Harriet's sister-in-law, and that the other Martin girl had married and moved away. Mr. and Mrs. Robert Martin had few servants and as it was harvest time, even those might not be about. She tested the door; it was not locked; she pushed it open and stepped inside.

The room was not complete chaos, but nor was it the well-ordered space that Emma had visited on earlier occasions. A stained pinafore lay crumpled on a chair; a few dishes with crumbs on them needed to be cleared and washed; the pillows could use plumping, the furniture needed dusting and the floor needed sweeping, especially of dog hair. The dog who had been shedding came over to Emma, sniffing her hand and her basket of bread, recognizing her as a friend and then wagging its tail in greeting.

"Where is your mistress?" Emma asked the animal, speaking softly. Harriet was probably exhausted and could be asleep somewhere.

The dog seemed to understand her question, for it turned and led towards a hall in the back, its toenails clicking on the wooden floor. Emma put her basket down on a table and followed the animal and then peered hesitantly around the hall corner, softly calling, "Harriet?"

Unfortunately Harriet did not realize her friend was there and at the sight of someone unexpectedly in her home she shrieked and dropped the jug she was carrying. It dropped on the floor, shattered into many pieces, and water splashed everywhere.

"Oh! Mrs. Knightley, it is you," Harriet said, with an effort to be formal and polite, because Mrs. Knightley belonged to the best families of Highbury, which Harriet herself could not claim; even her husband, Robert Martin, was the tenant of Mrs. Knightley's husband. Their relative positions demanded deference. But then the situation overwhelmed Harriet and she simply burst into tears. "Oh, Mrs. Knightley!" she wailed.

Emma sprang into action. She asked Harriet several questions, determining what was most urgent, then told her to go to her crying children.

"I will take care of this," Emma said resolutely looking down at the shards of the jug.

"But Mrs. Knightley –" Harriet objected, for it was inappropriate for the great Mrs. Knightley to occupy herself with cleaning up a cottage.

"Go on," Emma said, and then as her friend went upstairs, called good naturedly after her, "I won't tell anyone if you don't."

But Emma thought it was pretty likely that Harriet would prattle about how Mrs. Knightley had come in and assisted her – and that Robert Martin, too, would see the fruit of her efforts. She did not want to seem inferior to the least scullery maid, so she spent a full fifteen minutes clearing away the broken jug, sweeping the floor, and dusting and generally straightening. Surveying the area and deciding that the results would not shame her, she wiped her hands on a towel, and went through the hall again, calling, "Harriet," more loudly.

"In here, Mrs. Knightley," answered Harriet, and Emma followed her friend's voice until she found her in the nursery with her two babies. Again, in this room, disorder was taking hold, but Emma resisted the urge to straighten up.

Harriet was sitting in a chair nursing one of the twins. "Mrs. Knightley, I'm so sorry," and her hair was uncombed and there were tears on her face. "I just can't seem to manage anything. Robbie here wants to eat every two hours, and Lizzie takes forever when she nurses. I'm not eating or sleeping myself, let alone dressing or washing, and I have never been so tired in my entire life."

Emma thought briefly of her own well-organized household, including her competent nursemaid Mary, one of the many fruits of a large annual income. Perhaps she should be more charitable towards Mrs. Elton, who also had a young infant, another boy. The child was known to be colicky and a poor sleeper, so perhaps the Eltons were also very tired.

"Then let me help you," Emma said. "Would you like some water? Perhaps some tea?" she asked, for although she had a wet nurse for her own child now, she had nursed George for a little while after he was born and knew how thirsty the procedure could make a woman. She recalled that Harriet had been fetching water, too, when Emma had surprised her, and given how exhausted and worn-out Harriet was – poor girl, she was only nineteen, but already losing her looks, and she had been so pretty – the jug of water had to be important or Harriet would not have made it a priority.

"Yes, but the jug's broken," Harriet said.

"I will find something," and Emma left the room. She rummaged in the kitchen, set the kettle on, and ended up surprising Sue, the milkmaid, nearly as much as she had startled the milkmaid's mistress. Sue managed not to drop anything, although she was a little horrified that Mrs. Knightley, such a great personage in Highbury, should actually speak to her. Nevertheless she gathered her wits and assisted Emma in finding a substitute jug, fetching water, and telling her where to find the tea things. In another twenty minutes Harriet had drunk some water, dried her tears, combed her hair and had even started to smile a little – which improved her looks immediately. Emma suggested they take the babies into the parlor, where the tea things were, and when Harriet arrived and saw the bread and the pastries laid out neatly on the table, she cried out, "Oh, Mrs. Knightley!" yet again.

After Harriet had eaten some food and drunk some tea, her color returned and her natural cheerfulness and sweet temper reasserted themselves.

Emma then apologized for having frightened her so badly. "My dear friend, I hope you are feeling a little better now."

"Oh, yes!" Words could not express the gratitude Harriet was feeling, but she tried, rather incoherently.

"I did not mean to startle you so," Emma continued, pouring Harriet a cup of tea.

"Oh, Mrs. Knightley, I know you didn't, but I frighten easily these days. And when I saw you – well, I didn't see *you*, for if I had known it was *you*, I certainly would not have been terrified. But these days I am often frightened, and I thought that a stranger had forced his way into the house."

Emma cut a slice of bread for her friend, buttered it, and passed it to Harriet, who ate it greedily and gratefully. "But Highbury is one of the safest places in England. Why should you think strangers are forcing their way into houses?"

"Because of the gypsies. Just yesterday I saw gypsies."

"Gypsies?" Emma asked.

Gypsies had come through Highbury before, and Harriet and a school friend of hers had been accosted by a gang. They had demanded money – Harriet had offered her small purse – but they had not been satisfied and had continued to threaten her. Only the fortuitous arrival of Mr. Frank Churchill on horseback had frightened them off; he had then escorted Harriet to Hartfield, depositing her with the Woodhouses and making sure she was well before he continued to London.

Emma recalled how Harriet had fainted that day and how considerate, how solicitous Mr. Frank Churchill had been. Yet perhaps it did not compare with the intense emotions that Harriet had experienced during her year of being in love with Mr. Robert Martin – then with Mr. Elton (and although Emma blushed at her role in that, Harriet had been very persuadable) – then with Mr. Knightley, a choice which also caused Emma some pain, but at least Harriet's unrequited passion had alerted Emma to her own feelings for Mr. Knightley.

But romance – courtship and passion – fade for some, and Emma wondered if Harriet were imagining gypsies out of a hope to add excitement to her humdrum albeit exhausting existence – or if Harriet's fatigue was itself yielding fevered imaginings. "Are you sure, Harriet?" Emma asked gently.

Of course she was sure! Harriet answered with some force and decision of character. Emma recalled how Mr. Knightley had once complimented her, Emma, for having improved Harriet's character in this regard. Emma thought that Harriet was a little firmer in her approach to life, but she did not think she deserved any credit for it. Emma thought it was more likely due to Harriet's being a little older, more experienced – and the mother of twins.

"There are gypsies working for Mr. Gilbert," Emma said, "perhaps you saw some of them?"

Harriet conceded it was possible, for she did not know everyone working at the Gilbert farm, but she expected that all Gilbert's help posed no danger, while she had sensed evil intentions in the people who had lurked behind her house.

"If you are afraid of intruders, I am surprised you did not lock your front door," Emma said.

Harriet said she had considered it – but since the strangers had appeared at the back, she had decided to leave the front open. What if she needed to escape quickly? She could never carry both her babies and unlock the front door.

Emma conceded mentally that this was a reason, although not necessarily the best. Harriet was obviously in a state and needed comfort instead of criticism. "Where did you see them? Were they the same ones who accosted you before?"

With Emma showing interest instead of doubt, Harriet was happy to share all the particulars of her experience, and pointed to the back gate where the people had lurked. The fact that they had not used the road in front of the house was itself suspicious.

"And you were alone? Completely alone?" Emma inquired

"Except for the babies," said Harriet. "Mrs. Martin and Elizabeth are away; Robert was in the field; and Sue was milking the cows when I saw them. Mrs. Knightley, I'm just not accustomed to seeing strangers there and they frightened me. One of them laughed at me, and I am sure the others wished me ill."

"Did your dogs bark?" asked Emma.

"The dogs that bark were away with Robert. I don't like them in the house – they're so large compared to the twins. I don't think they're dangerous, but they always lick my babies' faces. I only kept Ginger here for company; she's too sweet to bark at anyone."

Emma then asked what had happened. It took a while to elicit the information from Harriet, who was reliving the terror she had felt at the time, but Emma finally learned that the gypsies – whoever they were – continued without causing any noticeable damage. They were gone several hours before Harriet's husband returned from taking care of his sheep, but even he saw the footprints before the gate.

"He saw footprints before the gate?" repeated Emma. This detail gave credence to Harriet's story, which Emma had been doubting. "Did you study them yourself?"

"No, Mrs. Knightley, since I never saw the gypsies' feet and don't know what sort of shoes they were wearing, I did not think it would do any good. Besides, I was too frightened to go outside. I've been nervous ever since, but Robert can't stay with me every minute."

"It does not look frightening," remarked Emma, staring out the window. The scene was as bucolic as anyone could wish: a dozen chickens in their coop, a few buildings, buckets and a pitchfork. The garden looked like many kitchen gardens in early autumn, with the spikes of onions still sticking out of the ground, turnips and parsnips likewise showing their tops, a few pumpkins giving color to the bed, whereas the leaves from other vegetables such as runner beans which had already been harvested and stored in jars for the coming winter were starting to wither. Beyond the gate, which appeared so innocent from where she stood, were a few trees and some shrubbery. The trees were a mixture of spruce and birch; the latter's leaves already sprinkled with gold. She did not understand how Harriet could have declined investigating, especially if her husband Robert was with her to protect her.

"No, it doesn't, does it? It is the middle of the day, but now I am afraid to stir out of my own front door. Or rather, my back door," Harriet amended.

"Do you mind if I take a look?" Emma asked, putting the twin she was holding on the sofa beside Harriet, and then pulling on her cloak.

"Are you not frightened?" asked Harriet, her blue eyes wide. "Of course you are not, Mrs. Knightley; what am I thinking? You are not a weak-spirited creature like myself."

"Nonsense, you are not weak-spirited," Emma said, although she had been thinking that very thing about Harriet just a moment before. "You are not sleeping because of the babies, and that makes you fanciful. And although I am as frail as you are, I can see from here that no strangers are around, and as you say, it is the middle of the day. Besides, my coachman James will hear me if I cry out."

Despite Emma's reassurances, Harriet's terror was so great that Emma could not help absorbing some of her friend's fear as she opened the door and walked out into the yard, and she had to repeat her own arguments to encourage herself to continue. The dog Ginger, usually indoors with Harriet, bounded outside with her. Emma was relieved for its company as she went over to the much-maligned gate, whose hinges needed oiling. She glanced back in the direction and waved. In the bright sunlight it was virtually impossible to see inside the cottage, but she hoped that if Harriet were watching, her confident smile – she tried to smile confidently – would reassure her friend.

The air was crisp but the sun was strong. Emma kept an eye out on the thick, overgrown shrubbery – it would be possible for someone to be hiding in it – but that person would have to be hiding in the bushes for some time now, without making a sound, and to what purpose? She looked at the ground and although there was evidence of footprints, it was impossible for her to tell how many, when they had been made – presumably since the last rain four days ago – or who had made them.

Emma went around to the front of the house, spoke to James and asked if he had seen anyone. The coachman said he had seen the milkmaid Sue, and from a distance, a shepherd tending his sheep and what looked like Robert Martin in his field – but no strangers and nothing suspicious. She told James she would be a while longer, and went back inside to Harriet, who was greatly relieved that Mrs. Knightley had come back inside – accompanied by the dog Ginger – completely unharmed.

Did you recognize anyone? How many people did you see? Can you describe them? To these questions Emma received no coherent, confident answer – there might have been two people, there might have been three, or even more, as the gate blocked the view and Harriet had been too frightened to look out the window for more than a short time. Still, Harriet was adamant on two points. She had seen someone, or some ones, and that occurrence had terrified her. She was certain something was wrong; that the unknown persons had had evil intent. Yet whoever it was had not taken anything; Harriet could say this because her husband Robert had looked through everything, going around the house and checking the animals and the outer buildings as well.

Emma recalled that Mrs. Weston's turkeys had been pilfered several years ago and mentioned that to her friend.

"Just so!" cried Harriet.

Emma was surprised that, given how anxious Harriet was, that Mr. Martin had left Harriet to herself.

"I did not want him to go, but it is the middle of the day and there is the harvest – the harvest cannot wait. Besides, as you see, they appear to have cleared off – Robert looked everywhere. Besides, again, Sue is with the cows and Tom," – a sallow-faced youth who helped with the harvest – "is sometimes on the property so I am not quite alone. And if there was someone bad in the area, then going to Donwell Abbey sooner rather than later was necessary, so Robert is planning to go to see Mr. Knightley this afternoon – he could be there now. Mr. Knightley could hardly arrange to get rid of the bad people if he does not know they exist."

"I cannot argue with you," said Emma, because this time Harriet's reasoning was fairly sound – and when it was not, arguing was likewise out of the question. She also felt a swelling of pride in her husband, at how everyone in Donwell and Highbury turned to *him* to solve problems.

One of the babies sneezed and waved its small fists and Emma judged it was time to change the subject. They discussed the fact that Harriet was expecting again; the joyful event was still seven months away. They spoke of Mrs. Martin, and the letter she had sent from Bath and how she and her daughter Elizabeth were enjoying the Pump Room. And the latest gossip – Elizabeth Martin, Harriet's sister-in-law, was being courted by William Cox, a lawyer. "Mrs. Martin thinks Elizabeth should accept William Cox's proposal, but Elizabeth wants to think about it."

They briefly discussed the death of Mrs. Bates: "Miss Bates must be so sad!" Harriet exclaimed, and for a moment looked sorrowful and sympathetic, until the other child woke and began to wail at which point she returned to her own concerns.

Emma judged Harriet was in a better mood and that she had done all she could for her for the time being. The milkmaid was back inside, and so Harriet was not quite alone. "Will you be all right if I depart? I must continue to Donwell Abbey."

"Oh! Yes!" Harriet thanked Emma over and over for her visit, the assistance and the basket of provisions, and said that Mrs. Knightley had done her a world of good. "You are so kind to me."

"Try to get some rest, dear Harriet," Emma advised, although she did not know how or if her young friend would be able to follow such advice.

"Yes. Rest more, of course," Harriet repeated, and then yawned so grandly that Emma thought young Mrs. Martin might fall asleep then and there. Emma made sure the twins were not in danger of falling or harming themselves in any other way, then put on her cloak and departed.

James helped her into the carriage and then climbed up himself and started. Before they were more than five minutes away from the Martin cottage, Robert Martin himself came around the bend in the lane. Emma tapped on the roof to signal for the carriage to stop, then lowered the window and called out to him.

"Mrs. Knightley," Robert Martin acknowledged, bowing slightly.

"Robert Martin," said Emma, who was relieved for this manner of meeting, which would force them to keep their meeting short. Emma and Robert Martin had never moved in the same circle; his status in Highbury was both too low for her to notice and yet too high for her assistance. Robert Martin naturally resented Emma's influence, as Harriet's refusal of his first proposal had delayed his present happiness for almost a year.

So, they had no reason to be friends, and even some reason for animosity; still, Emma was glad to see him. His return would greatly reassure his wife. They exchanged greetings and Robert Martin reported to her that he had spoken with Mr. Knightley and so far there had been no more sign of any gypsies.

"But you are sure someone was there," Emma persisted, who continued to doubt Harriet's story, as those footprints could have made any time, by anyone.

"Yes, someone was there," said Robert Martin.

"Thank you. Your wife will be glad to see you," she said, and Robert Martin reciprocated with the observation that her husband would be glad to see *her*. It was as if neither could understand their partners' unaccountable taste, but did not deny it was so.

She waved farewell; he awkwardly inclined his head, then she let James know he should continue. The horses clopped forward, and the carriage rolled on. The road was fairly good between the Abbey-Mill Farm and Donwell Abbey. She scanned for suspicious gypsies – looking left and right – but except for a few crows pecking some apples on the ground and a flock of sheep in the distance, she saw no one more alarming than William Larkins.

She thought with satisfaction of her visit to Harriet. Emma felt she had done all she could for her friend during her short visit. She had offered her moral and practical support; she had brought bread and honey and had made her tea. Still, Harriet – sweet and indecisive Harriet – needed more substantial assistance during this difficult time. The best scheme would be a girl to help, at least part time, with some of the work, but Emma did not know of anyone suitable and was not sure if she could suggest such a thing to the Martin household. Robert Martin might not be able to afford it, and if Emma tried to offer temporary assistance, he still might object out of pride. She would have to think of some way to arrange it.

In the meantime she was resolved to send over another basket of bread and some nourishing stew the next day – easy fare, quick to prepare – and to include with the provisions a new jug to replace the one she had startled poor Harriet into shattering.

6 CARRIAGE RIDE TO HARTFIELD

Emma had spent more time at the Abbey-Mill Farm than she expected, so by the time that she reached Donwell Abbey the sun was low in the sky. If they wanted to return to Hartfield before her father started to worry – and they both knew how easily Mr. Woodhouse worried, especially about his precious daughter – they had to depart at once. Mr. Knightley was disappointed not to be able to show his wife the improvements being made to his cider press. Donwell Abbey, like so many former monasteries that had become estates, was famous for its apple orchards, and Mr. Knightley was always interested in finding a way to improve the output of his trees and find other uses for his fruit.

Emma appreciated good cider, but she had never thought much about the work that went into making it: tending trees, picking the fruit, sorting them, then crushing them until the juice flowed, and she could only muster moderate enthusiasm for the process. She apologized for being late but said they needed to get home to her father and their baby.

Mr. Knightley, in a good humor because the harvest looked promising, nevertheless sighed as he settled into the Woodhouse carriage. Emma knew it was hard for him to leave Donwell Abbey every day – she tried to look at it as *her* future home, which of course it was, but she still felt a strong attachment to Hartfield. She wondered if she had inherited some of her father's character after all, for her father's preference for his own home was very strong – or if she just wanted to return to Hartfield because her father and her son were currently there, and if in her later life she would be just as attached to Donwell Abbey as she was now to Hartfield.

Although Mr. Knightley disliked departing from his estate, he knew he would return the next day – or the day after that, as on the morrow there was the funeral for Miss Bates – and so he was able to depart with tolerable equanimity. His sigh, although interpreted by his wife as reluctance, was due more to fatigue, for the day's work had been strenuous. Mr. Knightley was actually relieved to be returning comfortably in his wife's carriage, especially as James and the horses would take him more quickly than his own two feet to warm fires, a good dinner – Mr. Knightley would never admit it to Hodges, his cook at Donwell Abbey, but Serle, the Hartfield cook, was better – and his child. After failing to interest wife in the improvements he was making to his cider press, he inquired after the health and spirits of her friend.

The topic of Harriet Martin was more interesting to Mrs. Knightley than the details of farming. She was eager to know what Robert Martin had told him about Harriet's sighting of gypsies. Did Mr. Knightley, after speaking with Robert Martin, think that Harriet was in any danger?

Mr. Knightley told Emma what he and Robert Martin had discussed, and the account given by Mr. Knightley was consistent with what Harriet had told Emma – which was not surprising, as both originated with that young matron. Mr. Knightley was convinced, because Robert Martin was convinced, that Harriet Martin had seen someone or some people at the back gate, but whether she had sighted strangers – and especially dangerous strangers – could not be determined.

"Do you think Harriet could be imagining danger?" Mr. Knightley asked as the coach turned along a curve and then went downhill.

Emma considered. She did not think Harriet would deliberately invent something fearful, but Harriet's power of observation was not the most acute. Harriet was extremely overtired, and it was possible that in her fatigued state, that she had failed to recognize friends, or that she had simply been unnecessarily alarmed by strangers.

"I agree. From Martin's description, it could have been as simple as some people losing their way, and wanting to ask for direction."

"But why would they come to the back and not the front?" Emma inquired.

Perhaps no one had answered the front gate, or perhaps they were simply crossing the field.

Emma had a few other ideas. Perhaps one of the servants at Abbey-Mill Farm was expecting friends or acquaintances, and these people were not known to Harriet. Or perhaps Elizabeth Martin had an admirer who did not realize that she was away in Bath – or perhaps Harriet had a secret admirer. After speculating on possibilities, she asked Mr. Knightley what action, as a local magistrate, he would take.

"We will keep an eye out for suspicious strangers, but even if someone trespassed along that path," – for that path was private property – " that path is so commonly used that it would be wrong to make a case against anyone, even if they were trespassing."

They discussed whether or not to inform Mr. Woodhouse of the sighting of potential strangers. Although Emma enjoyed the mystery and the prospect of excitement, the Knightleys knew that these very qualities would injure Mr. Woodhouse's tranquility.

Emma considered. She did not like to keep anything from her father, partly because he could find out anyway, but she agreed that, from the way Mr. Knightley put it, it could be a fuss about nothing. Besides, she reflected silently, worrying her father with the prospect or possibility of gypsies could make it more difficult for *her* to go about when and if she wanted to. Not that she was concerned for her own sake – the roads to Randalls and to Highbury were short and well-traveled – but she did not want to distress her father.

"Very well, we will not mention it and we will be reassuring if anyone else does. What topic should we choose to amuse my father?"

Harriet's fatigue, they decided, would be the best subject for diverting Mr. Woodhouse. Mr. Woodhouse enjoyed any description of ill-health, and fatigue was a close relative to illness – but without the morbid association with death – and as Mr. Woodhouse had always been fond of Harriet, and as he was gentle and generous in his way, he could enter into schemes for finding ways to relieve her from his exhaustion. Mrs. Bates's funeral, scheduled for the morrow, could not be avoided but they would have to touch upon it with delicacy.

"I am worried about you, Emma," said Mr. Knightley, as the carriage rumbled through Hartfield's iron sweep-gate.

"About me? But why?" asked Emma, surprised that anyone could consider *her*, healthy, wealthy, and a happily married mother with a little boy, to be an object of concern. "Do I not seem in good health and good spirits?"

"You are the picture of excellent health and the embodiment of good spirits," said Mr. Knightley, with a smile. But then, with more seriousness, he continued. "And you have a lively mind – a mind which I fear has been too confined by circumstance."

"Really," said Emma, pondering her husband's observations, as the carriage pulled to a halt before the entrance.

"I think it explains your tendency to extend your imagination in other areas," said Mr. Knightley. He opened the carriage door, descended, then turned and waited to help her out.

"You believe that I am spending too much time wondering about the people who may – or who may not have – passed Harriet's back gate. Or even the Eltons' finances."

"These things are harmless enough," said Mr. Knightley, "but you, who have so much intelligence and imagination, deserve a better scope for your powers."

"Such as?" Emma asked, curious. She nodded at James, who drove the carriage and the horses towards the stable.

"Ah, my dear, if only I knew! It would help if you were interested in farming."

"Does that require much imagination?" asked Emma.

"Sometimes," said Mr. Knightley.

Mr. and Mrs. Knightley then proceeded through Hartfield's front door, opened for them by the butler, who took her coat. The butler then handed her a note from the Westons. In it Mrs. Weston satisfied Emma's curiosity by letting her know that Mr. and Mrs. Churchill had indeed come down from London for Mrs. Bates's funeral. Also, given that the Westons had guests, and that they would be attending the service in the morning themselves, would Emma explain to dear Mr. Woodhouse that she and little Anna Weston would not be calling the following morning?

As they entered the parlor to greet Mr. Woodhouse, sitting before his fire, Emma wondered at her own lack of imagination, for self-pity had never entered any of her fantasies. As she took a seat beside her father, her life seemed rich enough to her. She had friends and she had family and she had enough money – not just to provide herself with a comfortable life, but enough to be generous and to assist her friends.

7 THE FUNERAL OF MRS. BATES

For more than two decades, the name *Mrs. Churchill* had been hated in Highbury, for Mr. Weston's late wife's sister-in-law was the subject of many complaints. *Mrs. Churchill* was the one whose pride and jealousy had prevented the handsome young Frank Churchill from spending any time in Highbury. *Mrs. Churchill* had invented illnesses, had demanded attention from her nephew, and had been an obstacle to his making plans for his future. She was considered an especial hindrance to his choosing a wife, because her pride and jealousy would have certainly found something terribly wrong with any young lady chosen by her nephew, and she was known for her influence over her husband, who allegedly held the purse strings. Although several women in Highbury were considered by one faction or another as suitable brides – Emma Woodhouse by the Westons and many others, and Harriet Smith by Emma Woodhouse herself – an actual marriage with Mr. Frank Churchill was deemed impossible, because *Mrs. Churchill* would do everything to prevent it.

Those living in Highbury considered Mrs. Churchill as a hindrance to the future happiness of their favorite tended to dismiss her illnesses and pains as mere caprice. Then she died, quite suddenly in Richmond. Those in Highbury could not pretend to feel sorrow – even though none save Mr. Weston and his son had ever met her in the flesh, they had hated her in spirit too long to grieve – although a few who were more alert to their tendencies to self-contradiction acknowledged that perhaps her long-mentioned illnesses and sufferings had been genuine instead of imaginary. But Highbury did not have much time to examine its collective conscience and berate itself for its tendency to judge at a distance. Shortly after that, the startling news came out: Mr. Frank Churchill and Jane Fairfax were engaged! Long engaged! Secretly engaged! Everyone was surprised, terribly surprised.

Since then Jane and Frank had married and so the former Miss Fairfax was now the current Mrs. Churchill. The name which for so many years had been mentioned with distaste was now uttered with pleasure and pride. Nowhere was this more evident than in Mr. Weston, who had suffered the most from the haughtiness of the first Mrs. Churchill.

"They have come," Mr. Weston announced outside the church to the Knightleys, as Mr. Woodhouse and Mr. and Mrs. Knightley approached the church, in their most somber attire, to attend Mrs. Bates's funeral. "They have come in their own carriage, and have just used it to fetch Miss Bates from her apartment. Yes, they have come," he announced to the next arrivals, the Coles, "even though Jane has not been well since—" and then he stopped speaking.

Many weddings had occurred among the Highbury principals in the last two years: Anne Taylor had become Mrs. Weston; Augusta Hawkins was now married to Highbury's vicar, Mr. Elton; Harriet Smith had accepted Mr. Robert Martin; and of course Emma Woodhouse had become the bride of Mr. George Knightley. These pairings had all been blessed with children. Jane Fairfax's union with Mr. Frank Weston Churchill was the only one without offspring. Hopes of a child had been rumored several months ago, followed by bitter disappointment and concern for Jane Churchill's safety. Miss Bates had not been able to keep silence on the matter, of course, and her worries about the health of her niece had been shared with all the women in Highbury.

"Of course," said Emma Knightley, forestalling Mr. Weston from venturing into what was usually strictly female territory. Mr. Weston was an open-hearted man, also not known for keeping quiet. The child in question would have been his own grandchild, so naturally in this subject his heart and his words flowed almost as readily as Miss Bates's.

Mrs. Weston caught her husband's arm and squeezed it, which also helped stanch the flow of words, and Mr. Weston more soberly accepted the Coles' congratulations on the return of his son and daughter-in-law to Highbury. Emma's lips twitched as she repressed a smile; it was difficult to feel a great deal of sorrow at the death of a woman who had lived well beyond her three score years and ten, and she could understand that for Mr. Weston the occasion offered more joy than grief. Mr. Knightley said they looked forward to seeing Mr. and Mrs. Churchill, either at Randalls or at Hartfield, when circumstances allowed it. Then they turned to Mr. Woodhouse and assisted him inside.

Highbury's church was one of the few places that Mr. Woodhouse would go to outside of his own house. If Mr. Woodhouse did not attend services once a week, as he did most Sundays, an excursion to the parish church would have been too great a departure from his usual habits to ask of him, even for the sake of burying his old friend Mrs. Bates. But as Mr.

Woodhouse attended church Sundays and holidays, it was possible for him to come on this weekday, and to take his usual place in his pew.

The funeral was attended by all who were expected. There were a few doddering old women who remembered the aged Mrs. Bates when she was young, and many others of middling years who recalled her when she was a hale and hearty matron. Most people came to support Miss Bates and to get a glimpse of the Churchills. While Highbury pressed its way into the church, Emma was pleased that the position of the Woodhouse pew gave her plenty of opportunity to study the visitors from London. Although she certainly preferred Mr. Knightley to any other man, there was no denying the fact that Mr. Frank Churchill was tall and good-looking, to a degree rarely seen in Highbury, and hence a guilty pleasure to observe.

"No one was more beloved than your grandmamma, my dear," Miss Bates said to her niece Jane Churchill, leaning on her nephew-in-law's strong arm, while mourners continued to fill the pews in the back.

"No, Aunt," said Jane, whose wan face bespoke sorrow. Her clothes were finer than they had been in the past – she wore the most elegant black crepe that a large income could buy – but Emma thought Jane did not look happier than she had when she had lived in Highbury about a year ago. Back then, Jane had been troubled by the uncertainties in her future, but she must have been delighting in the knowledge of her secret engagement to Frank Churchill, Emma mused. Then Emma was overcome by shame: who was *she* to judge Jane Churchill? Why on earth should Jane Churchill appear happy just now? It was, after all, a funeral – the funeral of Jane's dear grandmamma, who had raised her when she was little and had loved her all her life. How sad would she, Emma, feel when her own father died? How wan would she look?

"A fine wreath sent by the Campbells, and flowers from the Dixons," Mrs. Elton whispered to Mrs. Cole, but so loudly that others could hear.

Under lowered lashes, Emma studied Mrs. Elton, her serious reflections usurped by her curiosity about her foe. She thought Mrs. Elton was more pleased with herself than usual – which was saying something – but decidedly, the vicar's wife had a greater than normal air of contentment. Was it merely because she *was* the vicar's wife, and hence enjoying a role of importance at this funeral, certainly the most significant event of the season in Highbury, thanks to the appearance of the Churchills? Or had something else happened to contribute to her self-satisfaction?

Mr. Elton came out in his surplice and began the service. It was a proper funeral for a proper vicar's wife – solemn, but not overly sad, except for her daughter and her granddaughter. Miss Bates wept – she did not sob aloud, but tears streamed down her face – and Jane Churchill's lips trembled as she supported her aunt.

Mr. Elton made a point of mentioning Mrs. Bates's connection to the church – where she had spent decades as the vicar's wife – and what a mainstay she had been to the Highbury parish. During this reference Emma saw Mr. Elton glancing briefly at his wife, and Mrs. Elton giving a tight little nod of approval; evidently the Eltons had decided it was more important to praise Mrs. Bates in front of her wealthy granddaughter than it was to pretend that Mrs. Elton was the epitome of vicar's wives.

The procession from the church to the freshly dug grave was short. Mr. Elton, as the vicar, was in the lead, followed directly by Mrs. Bates's coffin, which was carried by Mr. Weston, Mr. Frank Churchill, Mr. Cole and Mr. Knightley. Next came the principal mourners: Mrs. Bates's daughter, Miss Bates, and Mrs. Bates's granddaughter, Jane Fairfax Churchill. After that it was a matter of Highbury precedence: Mrs. Knightley, of course, Mrs. Weston, Mrs. Elton and Mrs. Cole and then the village's lesser denizens, including the Perrys and the Coxes and Mrs. Goddard, the local schoolmistress.

The plain casket was lowered into the grave, next to the casket in which Mr. Bates himself had been buried nearly thirty years before. The neat churchyard, with the dappled sunlight shining through the spruce trees, was a pretty place to rest, thought Emma, supporting her father's arm as Mr. Elton intoned a prayer. A young maid, one of the Cole daughters, came forward rather self-importantly with a basket of small evergreen branches; everyone trailed by and took one and tossed it into the grave, then paused to say a word to Miss Bates.

Afterwards, many of the mourners went to a reception at the Crown Inn. Some might find it odd for a minister's widow to be celebrated in an inn, but Miss Bates's apartment was too small, and the Crown Inn was such a fixture in Highbury – its owners so respectable – that no one except the very retiring Mr. Woodhouse could make any objection. Whenever there was a funeral or important occasion for which the resident did not have adequate space and that resident had sufficient funds to hire the Crown Inn, the Crown Inn was engaged. The bread and cold meats were supplied at a distance by the Campbells, who had raised Jane as their own and so had been a friend of Mrs. Bates for many years.

So it was in the Crown Inn that the principals met again, drinking sherry and eating. Mr. Knightley, aware of time being spent away from the harvest, only stayed long enough to offer condolences to the principals, and then used the Woodhouse carriage to go to Donwell, where he would change into farming clothes. Emma and her father remained in the Crown, waiting for the carriage to return and to take them back to Hartfield. Her father had insisted on coming, thinking that he would be strong enough, and had expressed his condolence to Mrs. Churchill and to Miss Bates in person as Mrs. Bates had been a lifetime friend. Both ladies were sensible of the honor being done, but after voicing his gentle sorrow and eating a very little piece of bread – Mr. Woodhouse stayed away from the meats, for he did not trust the cooks at the Crown Inn, despite their having fed nearly half of Highbury at one point or another to no ill effect – Emma had to find him a place near the fireplace to sit, and to distract him until their carriage returned from delivering Mr. Knightley to Donwell Abbey. At first Mr. Woodhouse kept himself busy by staring at all the people and the room itself – into which he had hardly stepped during his life – but soon the novelty and wonder of his being in a different room began to fade.

"It is not warm enough," Mr. Woodhouse objected. "This great room is too drafty."

"Then, Papa, why don't we move your chair a little closer to the fire. Is that better?"

"I suppose." The old man frowned. "Do you think James will return soon? But the horses must be tired. They will walk very slowly."

"Dear Papa, I don't think the horses will mind pulling the carriage to Donwell and back. They are not like people – they can go much further than people without getting tired."

"Mr. Woodhouse, how considerate of you to come." That was Mrs. Weston, who, from her many years living at Hartfield, could see when Emma needed a little assistance in keeping Mr. Woodhouse occupied. "Your appearance means a great deal to Miss Bates and Mrs. Churchill."

Mrs. Weston sat down beside Mr. Woodhouse, and Emma took advantage of her friend's presence to rise to go to the window to look and see if the carriage was coming. She stepped behind a curtain, and after a moment two people moved closer to her, speaking in low voices, apparently not realizing she could hear. The voices belonged to Mr. and Mrs. Churchill.

"You know I must return to my uncle tomorrow," said Frank Churchill. "Are you sure you wish to stay in Highbury?"

"Yes," said Jane, "my aunt needs me now. Besides, I need to help her sort through my grandmother's things."

But how long could that take? Emma wondered. Mrs. Bates had owned very little and Jane Churchill struck her as very methodical. Miss Bates, too, despite her talkative nature, was orderly in her habits.

"Then why not stay with my parents? They would be happy to have you stay with them at Randalls, and it would be much more comfortable for you. I, too, would be happier knowing that you were warm and dry and had more servants at hand."

Emma silently concurred with Frank Churchill that living with the Westons would be far more pleasant than staying with Miss Bates and her apartment of only three rooms.

"You need not be concerned about me, Frank," Jane said. "I have lived with my aunt and my grandmother in the past, and now that my grandmother is – gone – there will be more room for me. Besides, I don't think my aunt realizes the emptiness she will feel. My aunt has spent the last years taking care of her mother, and if she is alone too long she will suffer."

Emma, unable to help overhearing, tried to swallow her disappointment. If *she* could choose which Churchill were to spend time in Highbury, she would definitely select Frank Churchill instead of his wife Jane. Frank was amusing and charming while Jane, though lovely and talented, was terribly reserved. However, Emma's heart applauded, for she believed that Jane was right; Miss Bates *did* need her niece's attention now. It would be a sacrifice for Jane, and from the way he sounded, for Frank Churchill too, but it was the kindest attention that Jane Churchill could show. And what would become of Miss Bates in the future? Thanks to her niece's marriage, at least poverty did not loom, but the ever-busy Miss Bates would need something to do.

Recalling where she was, Emma glanced again outside, and ascertained that the Woodhouse carriage had still not come back from Donwell. She moved away from behind the window curtain, evidently surprising Mr. and Mrs. Churchill, who jumped a little at her sudden appearance.

"Mrs. Knightley!" exclaimed Frank Churchill. "We did not see you behind the curtain."

"My apologies," Emma said, thinking that she was making a habit of coming unawares upon others. "I did not mean to startle you or to listen to a private conversation, but I was looking for our carriage which has taken Mr. Knightley to Donwell. My father, you understand, is anxious to return to Hartfield."

Jane recovered her equanimity first. "We apologize to you. We were not discussing anything particularly private, only my intention to remain a little while in Highbury."

"Yes, I overheard," Emma confessed. "All of Highbury will welcome you, Mrs. Churchill, although it is unfortunate that your visit has been precipitated by such a sad event."

Frank reached his hand out to touch the curtain. "A very pretty hiding place! I must remember it if I ever want to eavesdrop on an important conversation – but it is our fault, as we moved to this part of the room, and as Jane said, it is of no consequence." He smiled at Emma, but she could not help feeling he was concerned that he had said something indiscreet – or that he had been about to do so, and that she had missed it. He turned back to his wife. "Very well, my dear, you always do what is right. You know that party I must attend – uncle is desperate to have me with him – but I will make sure you are comfortable and I want you to come back soon. As soon as you are ready, my father will certainly loan you his carriage, or you can always hire the carriage from the Crown."

"Of course, when grandmamma's things are settled and I am at ease about my aunt."

"Frank!" called Mr. Weston. "I have something I want to show you!"

Frank left them to examine a painting on the wall of the Crown Inn – it showed a local stream that had been Mr. Weston's favorite fishing spot as a boy – and Emma felt that she could finally properly address Jane. She offered condolences on the death of her grandmother.

"You are very kind," Jane replied, her eyes shining with unshed tears; for once Emma felt that the lovely and accomplished Jane Fairfax Churchill was not hiding behind a wall of reserve. "How is your father, Mrs. Knightley?"

But Mrs. Elton usurped Mrs. Churchill's attention before Emma could reply. "Jane – my dear Mrs. Churchill – your aunt says you plan to stay with her for a while in Highbury. Mr. Elton and I are so looking forward to spending more time with you. And my little boy Philip – you will be absolutely delighted with him, I assure you. Of course, all of us mothers think our children are perfect, but I think you will find him especially charming."

Mrs. Churchill murmured something about looking forward to seeing Mrs. Elton's baby and, trying to be inclusive, politely added that she looked forward to seeing Mrs. Knightley's little son, too.

"Oh, little Knightley can't even sit up on his own yet," said Mrs. Elton, and then as if she had realized she had gone too far – Mr. Woodhouse was a large donor to the church – she continued with an affected laugh, "I'm sure he will in a month or two but infants are not so interesting until they do, are they?" She rapidly changed the subject: "Jane, as long as you're here, we would be happy to lend you our carriage if you and your aunt should need it," Mrs. Elton continued, and then, putting her hand on Jane's shoulder, drew her away. "Although Mr. E is going up to London tomorrow – he meant to go a few days ago, but stayed for your grandmother's funeral. But after that our coach and our horses will be at your disposal."

"Mr. Elton is going to London?" asked Emma politely. "To visit his mother and his sisters?"

"Yes. Mrs. Elton – I mean my mother-in-law, not myself – is considering moving in with one of her daughters and wants to get rid of some of things. There is a piece of furniture to which Mr. E is particularly attached – it belonged to his father – and Mrs. Elton will no longer have room for it."

"I see," said Emma, for Mrs. Elton seemed to be addressing her especially with this information. "It is very good of Mr. Elton's sister to offer a home to her mother."

"I suppose," said Mrs. Elton. Then, as if she had lost interest in the topic that she herself had introduced, she changed the subject. "Jane, as long as you are in Highbury, I thought we might organize some musical afternoons. I have a special little project I wish to discuss with you." And adroitly Mrs. Elton pulled Jane away, in another direction, leaving Emma alone before the curtained window.

Emma was annoyed, but did what she could to repress her irritation with Mrs. Elton. The vicar's wife had the right to claim greater intimacy with Jane Churchill than Emma could, as during Jane's last stay in Highbury she had shown the then-Miss-Fairfax far more attention. True, Mrs. Elton had caused some significant distress to Jane by trying to hurry her into a situation as a governess when Jane had implored her not to do so, but as Jane had let everyone know for years that she planned to be a governess and had never denied her intention to Mrs. Elton, Mrs. Elton's officiousness could be viewed as well-meaning if misdirected.

Emma glanced through the window again and this time she did see James and the carriage on its way. She relieved Mrs. Weston and collected her father. They made their slow way to the carriage – stopping to speak to Miss Bates, who, as she was surrounded by other friends, delayed them less than her volubility would usually allow – and then went home to Hartfield.

8 MUSINGS AFTER THE FUNERAL

Mr. Woodhouse, fatigued from the exertion of the funeral and his rare visit to the Crown, immediately sat in his chair before the fire and promptly took a nap. When he woke he was still tired and a little melancholy, so Emma resorted to playing backgammon with him to raise his spirits. By the time tea was ready – Mr. Knightley had returned and the baby, who was getting better at holding his rattle, was being passed around – Mr. Woodhouse's mood had improved and he was prepared to tell his son-in-law about his time at the Crown Inn.

"What will they do with Miss Bates, do you suppose?" Emma asked Mr. Knightley, as she poured them cups of tea.

"That is a good question," remarked her husband, picking up the rattle and grinning as he handed it to his son.

"What do you mean, what will they do?" Mr. Woodhouse asked.

"She took care of her mother for so long – she will miss her, sir, " Mr. Knightley explained. "Mrs. Bates has been the center of Miss Bates's life."

"Perhaps she will join the Churchills in London," Emma mused.

"You mean, Miss Bates will leave Highbury?" asked Mr. Woodhouse. "Why would she want to do that, and go to live in London, of all places?"

"Well, sir, to be with her niece."

"She had much better stay in Highbury," Mr. Woodhouse opined, who abhorred every sort of change. He had still not recovered from the marriage of his eldest daughter, Isabella so many years ago, and *her* removal to London.

"The Churchills are very well off," Emma reminded him. "Miss Bates might be more comfortable with them than in her current situation. It is not as if she would be leaving Hartfield, Papa, but a small apartment at the top of a long and narrow staircase."

"But – to leave Highbury! At her age! When she has spent her whole life here, and where all her friends live!" exclaimed Mr. Woodhouse.

"Perhaps you are right, sir, said Mr. Knightley. "It might be too great a change."

Mr. Woodhouse was so distressed by the possibility of Miss Bates leaving Highbury – at least Mrs. Bates, now that she was dead, would remain there permanently – that Emma was forced to find another subject. Again it involved travel to London, but this time she only mentioned that Mr. Elton was going there on the morrow to see his mother and his sisters.

This subject was much safer. Mr. Elton had not been in Highbury for decades; he was a relatively young man, and he traveled to London frequently enough for it not to be a shock to Mr. Woodhouse's delicate nerves. Besides, although Mr. Elton occasionally left, he always returned.

Will Mr. Elton go on horseback or take his carriage was a topic much more happily discussed than the possibility of Miss Bates permanently leaving her cramped, crowded apartment to go live in a spacious large house. Mr. Woodhouse was of the opinion that Mr. Elton should travel in his carriage, whereas Mr. Knightley believed that with such fine weather, riding would be far more efficient. Emma let the men discuss it at length and then mentioned that she understood that Mr. Elton was planning, in fact, to take his carriage.

Mr. Woodhouse sighed with relief, happy that Mr. Elton would be as comfortable as possible during the hours spent going to and from London, while Mr. Knightley frowned a little, as he, more aware of others than Mr. Woodhouse, thought also of the coachman, the extra horse needed to make the trip – one of Mr. Elton's horses tended to go lame – as well as the inconvenience it might prove to Mrs. Elton and her child while Mr. Elton was gone.

Mr. Woodhouse, however, did not see that Mrs. Elton's being without a carriage for a few days was such a great inconvenience. Where did she need to go? Everyone was safer at home.

Emma could have easily predicted both reactions, and was grateful that she was married to a man so considerate of his wife's mobility. She was, however, able to clear Mr. Elton of guilt in Mr. Knightley's eyes, by explaining to her husband that Mr. Elton was bringing back a piece of furniture that had belonged to his father. "I understand it will not fit on the back of a horse."

This excused Mr. Elton's behavior with Mr. Knightley, and increased the vicar's standing with Mr. Woodhouse, once he understood it. Although Mr. Woodhouse disliked the idea of people changing their homes, he minded it far less when furniture moved. The fact that the piece of furniture had belonged to Mr. Elton's father – and that Mr. Elton valued it because of it – was appreciated by Mr. Woodhouse.

"Very proper of him," sighed Mr. Woodhouse with approval. As he had never made the acquaintance of Mr. Elton's mother, and had barely even heard of her, the prospect of *her* moving from one house to another caused no consternation to him. They all discussed old furniture and possessions, and Mr. Woodhouse spoke at length about a chair of which he had been particularly fond, and a painted ball and cup that had been treasured by Emma. "Where do you think that ball and cup is now?"

"In Brunswick Square, Papa," said Emma. "The ball and cup belonged to Isabella, not to me, and is now a favorite plaything of her children."

"Ah, yes, of course," said Mr. Woodhouse, and lamented his poor memory, and complimented Emma on hers, and then they discussed having a small basin of gruel, which Emma then ordered, and a servant brought immediately.

After eating his gruel Mr. Woodhouse needed to be helped to bed and the baby began to fuss. It was not until the Knightleys had settled their charges for the night that they could continue their conversation, which they did in their rooms upstairs.

"So, Mrs. Churchill will be staying a while in Highbury," observed Mr. Knightley. "I am glad of it."

"I am sure Miss Bates will be very grateful," said Emma, pouring water from the ewer into the basin.

"There is no denying that Miss Bates will be grateful, and of course Jane is remaining here on account of her aunt, but that is not why I am glad."

Emma began to scrub her face. "Mrs. Churchill has always been a favorite of yours. She is so very musical."

"We all know that Mrs. Churchill is talented and I hope we will have the chance to listen to her play. But I was thinking more of her as a friend for *you*, Emma."

Emma frowned. "You are always encouraging me to be intimate with Jane Churchill. But Mrs. Elton is Mrs. Churchill's Highbury favorite – not me."

"Mrs. Churchill accepted Mrs. Elton's attentions in the past because no one else offered them to her. But the situation is different now and she might welcome a change."

"Perhaps," said Emma, rinsing the cloth in the water, and scrubbing some more. "I always thought that Mrs. Elton took a great interest in Jane Fairfax because it allowed her to feel superior – assuming that relative income is the only reason for superiority."

"It is true that men and women are usually esteemed for the size of their rents," Mr. Knightley said, picking up a book, putting it on his lap, but not opening it, "and I agree with you that Mrs. Elton may have befriended

Miss Fairfax because it allowed her to feel superior. If that is so, then Mrs. Elton will not be as eager for intimacy with Mrs. Churchill now."

"I think she will," said Emma, rinsing the cloth again, wringing it out, and then hanging it over the handle of the ewer to dry. She sat down beside Mr. Knightley on their sofa and explained how, at the Crown Inn, Mrs. Elton had pulled Mrs. Churchill aside in order to talk to her about planning a musical afternoon, deliberately excluding Emma from the conversation.

"So perhaps Mrs. Elton does not need to be richer than Mrs. Churchill in order to want to associate with her," Mr. Knightley concluded, "which contradicts your earlier supposition."

"You are right," Emma acknowledged, picking up a pillow case she was embroidering for the baby. "But I would never look to Mrs. Elton as an example of consistency. In the past I believe that Mrs. Elton befriended Miss Fairfax because she was poor – and now, absurd though it sounds, she wants to be friends with Mrs. Churchill because she is rich."

Mr. Knightley laughed. "My brother John would not want you in his law office!"

"I thought an advocate needed to be able to argue both sides."

"Very true, although I don't think John would recommend arguing both sides simultaneously. Well then, as I don't believe that you will advocate for Mrs. Elton" – and here Emma shook her head, so Mr. Knightley continued – "so in her absence, *I* will defend the vicar's wife. After all, even the worst offenders are entitled to counsel!"

"Pray continue," said Emma, as she threaded her needle.

"You say she took Mrs. Churchill aside to talk to her about organizing a musical afternoon, excluding you from the conversation?"

Emma pushed the needle carefully through the cloth. "Yes."

"We both acknowledge that Mrs. Churchill is musical, and so it stands to reason that Mrs. Elton would think that such an event would appeal to her."

Emma could not deny it.

"And did not Mrs. Elton, when she first arrived in Highbury, ask you to assist her in organizing these events?"

Emma pursed her lips but nodded. Mrs. Elton *had* made that very suggestion to her nearly two years ago. "My father could not bear so much activity," she said, carefully making a cross-stitch.

"Probably not," Mr. Knightley agreed, glancing down at his book. "But I think we can clear Mrs. Elton from the degree of rudeness you want to assign her. Perhaps instead of capital rudeness, she should only be charged with a misdemeanor."

"She insulted our son," Emma said.

Mr. Knightley's eyes opened wide. "No!"

"She did. She said Baby George is boring because he's still so little. She said her child is much more interesting."

"Then we'll hang her at dawn," joked Mr. Knightley. "Come, Emma, you can't fault a mother for preferring her child to ours. And, although I tease you for it, I will give you a compliment. I think your analysis of Mrs. Elton's relationship to Mrs. Churchill is accurate. I believe that Mrs. Elton enjoyed feeling superior to Miss Fairfax because it made her feel rich – just as she may want to continue the acquaintance now because Mrs. Churchill is rich."

Emma smiled and pushed the needle through the cloth.

"But before we condemn Mrs. Elton for choosing a companion because the friend made her feel superior, what about your friendship with Harriet Martin? Did you not spend time with Harriet Smith because the girl made *you* feel superior?"

This comparison was too apt to please Emma. She was assailed by especially unpleasant sensations, for in addition to feeling inferior to Jane Churchill – a burden she acknowledged – she was now suffering in comparison to the vain and pretentious Mrs. Elton! "There is some truth in what you say," she acknowledged. "But in my defense I must point out that when I first befriended Harriet, neither Mrs. Elton nor Mrs. Churchill were living in Highbury, and Mrs. Weston had just married Mr. Weston and had moved from Hartfield to Randalls."

"I agree, that at that time none of the young women in Highbury were your peers," Mr. Knightley acknowledged. "But this *is* your chance, Emma. Mrs. Churchill is the closest to an equal that you may ever see in Highbury – except for Mrs. Weston, who is nearly your mother."

Emma, making another cross-stitch, was touched by his concern. "At some point Mr. and Mrs. John Knightley will return to Hartfield," she said. As Isabella was the older daughter, when Mr. Woodhouse passed, the property would belong to her. "And then I will have my sister Isabella."

"Yes, but—" and then Mr. Knightley stopped, but Emma knew that although her husband loved her sister like a sister, and thought she made his brother an excellent wife, he did not consider Isabella Emma's intellectual equal.

"Very well," said Emma, preventing him from saying what neither of them wanted him to say. "As long as Mrs. Churchill is here, I promise to show her every attention. I will call on her and Miss Bates, and I will invite them both – and especially Mrs. Churchill – to Hartfield. But I cannot promise that my efforts will lead to a great friendship. We have had opportunities in the past, and it has never happened."

"An effort is all I ask, dear Emma."

"Was all well today at Donwell?" Emma asked, in an effort to change the subject to one that was less uncomfortable for her. "Were there other escaped bulls trampling your turnips? How many bushels of apples did you pick today? How many quarts of milk did your cows produce?"

"All is well at Donwell," said Mr. Knightley, opening his book. "How about if I read to you?"

He began to read to her, out of a book chosen from a list that Emma herself had made many years ago. She had never gotten beyond the novel's first chapter, but now it seemed, with Mr. Knightley for a husband, that she would no longer be able to put off improving her mind. Emma listened with one ear, but also had her own thoughts. She realized, as she sewed, that they had buried Mrs. Bates only that morning. How quickly some were forgotten, she thought, and then attended to the story Mr. Knightley was reading, which was more amusing than she had expected.

9 LOSING SILVER

The next morning the Knightleys and Mr. Woodhouse had barely begun their breakfast, when they learned that William Larkins was at the door. He occasionally walked to Hartfield to deliver a message to Mr. Knightley, but he had never appeared at such an early hour.

Emma stared at the fellow with alarm, for it seemed to her that only a catastrophe at the estate could explain Larkins's appearance.

"Yes, Larkins?" asked Mr. Knightley, tossing aside his napkin.

"Mr. Knightley, I have some news."

"Dear me," said Mr. Woodhouse, looking terrified; Emma reached over and took his hand.

"Tell me what it is, Larkins."

The young man spoke so slowly that Emma's fancy had time to dart everywhere. An accident in Brunswick Square, where the John Knightleys lived – Donwell Abbey burned to the ground – the pigs had started line-dancing in their pen...

The facts proved less extreme than her imagination, but Larkins's report was still serious. Thieves had broken into Donwell Abbey and had taken all the silver.

Mr. Woodhouse gasped, Emma felt her stomach sink, and Mr. Knightley's expression was grim as he rose to his feet. "Was anyone hurt?"

"No."

"How did they get in?"

"We're not sure."

Mr. Knightley shook his head. "Mr. Woodhouse, Emma, my love, I must go to Donwell directly."

"Of course," said Emma, and they quickly settled the practical matters, sending for the carriage which Mr. Knightley accepted without demur, and a promise on his part that he would let her know as soon as possible what was happening.

"Perhaps your friend Harriet saw some malcontents after all," said Mr. Knightley, too distracted to watch his words, and causing Mr. Woodhouse to fret. He saw what he had done, and apologized to Emma for his thoughtlessness.

"My love, I am sorry," he said, as Mr. Woodhouse sent away his morning gruel, too upset to eat any more than a bite.

"He would probably find out about them anyway," said Emma, glancing with concern over at her father – she was going to have a difficult morning and she gestured to the nursemaid that she should take the baby away. "You are worried about your house and your things," Emma said. "Go and take care of them. I will manage. We will be fine."

"But will you?"

"Yes, of course. There are plenty of servants and it is the middle of the day. Besides, Donwell Abbey would not have been broken into, I am sure, if you had been there." Emma was afraid that, looking at the distress on her husband's face, she had not sufficiently conveyed her appreciation of the sacrifice Mr. Knightley had made to live with them. She squeezed his hand. "I am grateful to you," she said. "Do not worry about my father – I can manage him."

Mr. Knightley glanced doubtfully over at the anxious Mr. Woodhouse, then stroked Emma's cheek. "I am sure you can. Thank you for your understanding."

Mr. Knightley departed with his man, William Larkins, and Emma turned to comforting her father.

"This is terrible. How can we go outside?"

"No need today, Papa. It looks like rain and would not be pleasant anyway."

"But what if the thieves come here? We need Mr. Knightley. And James has gone with them – the only person here who might protect us – sending him off with the carriage was a mistake."

Emma knew that attempting to change the subject would be impossible, and that Mr. Woodhouse's mood had to be endured until his normal spirits returned. She tried to reassure him by representing that people knew that Donwell Abbey was thinly staffed, and that its owner was never there at night, whereas everyone knew that Hartfield's owners were always at home. Her ideas did not comfort her father, however, for they suggested that people were watching the rich houses – and Hartfield, as the richest house in the neighborhood, would be watched the most.

"Perhaps you are right, Papa," said Emma and wondered if they should warn the other leading families of Highbury – especially the Coles, the Westons, and even the Eltons – about the break-in and robbery. Then she decided it was unnecessary; the information would spread rapidly, as did everything of note in Highbury.

"Harriet? What did you say earlier about Harriet?" Mr. Woodhouse inquired, proving that he had overheard part of the conversation between Emma and Mr. Knightley.

So Emma, as she feared, was forced to relate that Harriet had seen some strangers at the back of Abbey-Mill Farm but had no idea if they were involved. "They could simply be people who lost their way."

But Mr. Woodhouse became convinced that Harriet's strangers were responsible, that they had first watched Donwell Abbey and then had moved in the direction of Abbey-Mill Farm.

"It is possible," Emma conceded.

"What other explanation could there be? Do you think that Mr. Knightley's silver could have been stolen by someone who lives in either Highbury or Donwell?"

Put like that, Emma had to admit that the idea of someone familiar robbing the great houses in the area was especially unnerving. Still, in order to calm her father, she tried to minimize his fears. "Now, Papa, you know that William Larkins always exaggerates. Perhaps there has been a mistake."

"What sort of mistake could there be?"

Emma had to stretch her imagination to come up with a reasonable answer. She suggested that Mrs. Hodges, the cook, was no longer a young person. Perhaps she herself had moved the silver – in order to clean it – and had forgotten that she had done so.

"That is possible," Mr. Woodhouse said. "Just two days ago I could not find my slippers."

"So, it could all be nothing," said Emma. "We should not worry until Mr. Knightley returns with more information."

Excellent advice – Mr. Woodhouse agreed that they should not worry – but continued to do so anyway. Emma had hard work that morning – the backgammon table and even Baby George did not distract her father - and she could only hope that the day would pass quickly and that peace would be restored at Hartfield.

Emma sat down at the piano to amuse her son and her father, but had only played a few bars when they heard a bustle at the door. Mr. Woodhouse nearly jumped out of his chair, while Emma hoped – rather unreasonably, it was too soon – that Mr. Knightley had returned with a report on the situation. But the group that entered was entirely different: Mr. and Mrs. Weston had arrived with their little girl.

They had come because Mr. Knightley, on his way to Donwell, had stopped briefly at Randalls to let them know what had occurred at his estate. Mr. Weston said that they had heard and seen nothing, and asked if he should ride out with Knightley to Donwell to look things over. But Mr. Knightley said he had a different request: given the situation, his father-in-law was certainly anxious. Mr. Woodhouse would feel safer if Mr. Weston were in the house, and Mrs. Weston could assist Emma better than anyone else in offering Mr. Woodhouse a soothing word.

"I am most grateful," said Emma in a low tone to them both.

Mr. Knightley judged rightly; the arrival of Mr. Weston, who had been a captain in the militia when young, and who was known to still have his army pistol in a closet at home, even though he had not fired it in years, greatly lifted the spirits of Mr. Woodhouse. Furthermore, Mrs. Weston – less upset at the news of a theft at Donwell Abbey than Emma was – was better able to soothe her old friend and former benefactor. The antics of little girl and the baby, unaware of the events troubling the adults, finally amused Mr. Woodhouse despite himself.

As the day continued, the event became more interesting than terrifying, a great source of speculation and conversation, especially as Mr. Weston promised to remain with them until they received a message, at least, from Mr. Knightley. Word about the theft spread throughout Highbury, and throughout the rest of the morning and afternoon servants arrived bringing notes of concern from their neighbors: the Perrys, the Coles, Miss Bates and Mrs. Churchill, even the Eltons and Mrs. Goddard. They hoped that the Knightleys and Mr. Woodhouse were well; a few hinted that they would like more information whenever it became available. Emma and Mrs. Weston distracted Mr. Woodhouse by helping him compose and write responses to these neighborly inquiries; they were indifferent in their feelings, and they hoped to have more information later. The latter was especially useful, as it ensured that the next day or so would be occupied with more written exchanges with the rest of Highbury.

Mr. Weston, less interested in the correspondence, and no longer required to assume a protective pose to reassure Mr. Woodhouse, whiled away the time by playing with the children: helping his little girl, Anna, to walk around the room, much to the fascination of Emma's baby boy. With the latter Mr. Weston made funny faces, and the baby laughed merrily.

Emma ordered a basin of gruel for Mr. Woodhouse and tea and bread and cheese and cakes for everyone else. Everyone agreed with him that gruel was very healthful; none of the other adults would try any, but then little Anna Weston surprised everyone by asking for some and actually liking it. Mr. Woodhouse nodded his approval. "It is very good for you, Perry always assures me," he told Mrs. Weston, a statement he made a thousand times before, but Mrs. Weston nodded agreeably anyway. "She will not be bilious."

"Bilious?" objected Mr. Weston. "Of course not. My little Anna is as healthy as a – she is the picture of good health."

Before Mr. Woodhouse could continue enumerating the merits of gruel, and admiring little Anna Weston for liking it, they heard the front door open again. It was Mr. Knightley at last, and naturally all eyes turned towards him. Even the children stopped playing and looked up at Emma's tall husband.

"Well, Knightley?" asked Mr. Weston. "What happened?"

10 DETAILS FROM DONWELL

Mr. Knightley greeted Mrs. Weston, kissed his wife and child, shook hands with the men, then took a seat near the fire. Emma poured him a cup of tea and prepared him a plate with bread, butter and cheese, while everyone waited expectantly.

"Tell us what happened, Mr. Knightley," Mr. Woodhouse said. "Was it very distressing?"

Everyone listened as Mr. Knightley spoke. William Larkins had not erred; the silver was gone, truly gone, for they had searched the entire estate and had found nothing. Mrs. Hodges was nearly hysterical and he had needed time to calm her down. She had demanded that he inspect her rooms to prove that she was not guilty – he had never suspected her – but she demanded that he look through her rooms anyway. Once that was done, and nothing found, she was finally capable of giving intelligible answers to his questions.

With no master at Donwell Abbey, the silver was rarely used, only kept in a cabinet off the formal dining room – again a room, with Mr. Knightley residing at Hartfield, that was seldom visited. Mrs. Hodges made a point of polishing all the silver every month, dividing it into two groups and doing half each time. Hence she had not looked for the silver for an entire fortnight. Moreover, the thieves had only taken what was *inside* the cabinet, leaving several candlesticks and a tea set on display.

"Very clever," said Mrs. Weston, "the culprit did not want the theft to be detected."

"He wanted to maximize his time to get away," said Mr. Weston.

"My thoughts exactly," said Mr. Knightley.

Emma hesitated. She hated to say anything that might increase her father's anxiety, and yet she felt compelled to speak. "It does sound as if it was done by someone who knows some of the ways of Donwell Abbey."

"Indeed it does, Emma," said Mr. Knightley, and she could see that the idea had already occurred to him – and that he did not like it.

"A very bad business," said Mr. Woodhouse, "a very bad business."

"Can you tell us anything more?" asked Mrs. Weston, pulling her daughter, who was growing tired, on to her lap.

Mr. Knightley believed that the thief had broken through a side door, the one that led to the strawberry beds.

"No one picks strawberries at this time of year," said Mr. Weston. "Well, Knightley, do you have any suspects?"

Mr. Knightley shook his head. "I questioned Larkins and Hodges and the other servants, went over the grounds, and have even gone to my nearest neighbors to speak to them. Mr. Gilbert has plenty of help staying with him these days – such as that Draper fellow who helped with the bull – but Gilbert swears by them. I went to speak to Robert Martin and his family too. Harriet still maintains she saw some strangers, on the same day Gilbert's bull trampled my turnips."

The Westons asked when and how Gilbert's bull had invaded Mr. Knightley's turnips, and he succinctly explained it to them. Emma remarked to herself that the event, which had been so amusing when told before, now served only to remind them of when things had occurred.

"So do you think one of them could be the thief?" asked Emma.

"Harriet could not tell me much about the strangers, but one thing was certain – whoever she saw was on foot and not carrying anything. Donwell Abbey had a lot of silver, Emma. I don't see how thieves could carry it off without at least a cart of some sort."

Emma studied her husband; her heart went out to him. Mr. Weston, like usual, expressed himself openly. "A wretched loss, Knightley – a shame, a real shame. Anne, we should be getting home – the little girl is tired – Knightley, you'll let me know if there's anything I can do? I'm at your disposal."

It took the Westons a while to depart, with their farewells to Mr. Woodhouse and to Emma, and picking up their child. But eventually they left, with much gratitude on Emma's part for their assistance on a difficult day. The Hartfield inmates then ate their dinner, during which they continued discussing the situation at Donwell Abbey. Most of the anxious speculating was done by Mr. Woodhouse, who repeated his ideas and worries many times, and most of the reassuring was done by Mr. Knightley.

But Emma was sure that Mr. Knightley, out of concern for her father, was not voicing all of his thoughts. A glance at him, a slight nod from him, let her know that, like so often, they would discuss it later.

"So, Mr. Knightley," she said, when the others were asleep and they were settled in their room, "let me know what you really think."

"What more is there to say? Your father's right; it's a bad business – a very bad business."

"Tell me again how much is gone."

She listened – without picking up her needlework – as he told her. The thief had been thorough. Except for the items that were on display, all of Donwell Abbey's silver had been cleared out, including items that had been belonged to the Knightley family for two centuries. Moreover, the lock to the side door was broken – rather cleverly so, again not something one would notice. The loss, Mr. Knightley estimated, was worth many hundreds of pounds.

"I am so sorry," she said, for it struck her as a grievous loss. "Do you have any suspicions? Ones that you did not want to voice before my father?"

"Nothing definitive; but a few things seem more likely than others," said Mr. Knightley. "The thief must have had a means of conveying the silver, because there was too much for it to have been carried under someone's coat. Either there had been several people, or the thief had had a cart or a wheelbarrow or a carriage. And the theft must have happened during the last fortnight, since the last time Mrs. Hodges had cleaned the silver."

"Do you think it happened when that bull was in your turnip field?"

"It is tempting to think so, but does not strike me as likely. There were more people around – perhaps in a different part of the estate – but the thief would have been taking a great risk in entering Donwell Abbey when so many were running about. And strangers would not know where the silver was."

"Perhaps that was when the strangers determined *where* your silver was," said Emma.

"You are thinking of Gilbert's laborer, Draper," said Mr. Knightley.

She confessed that she was. "We know everyone else and it is hard to think you have been robbed by someone you trusted. Besides, if the door was damaged, it probably was not someone inside your house. Unless it was someone inside your house" – she contradicted herself a little, "and that person was trying to divert suspicion by damaging the door."

"It is unpleasant to think of anyone we know stealing the silver," Mr. Knightley admitted, "but Draper was not robbing me when he was helping to get the bull out of my field. I could see him most of the time, including when he was leading the animals away."

Emma tried to imagine the farmhand somehow hiding the Donwell Abbey silver somewhere about the animals before he left, but it was too difficult for even her practiced fancy. Where on the animals could he put the silver? How could he have managed it without the others noticing? Nay, it was impossible. "Perhaps he came back later," she said. "Perhaps he only used the bull's getting into your field as an excuse to look over your estate."

"Perhaps," said her husband. "But when I spoke to Draper at Gilbert's – and I made a point of speaking to him in his own lodgings, under the pretext of wanting to question everyone and ask if anyone had seen anything suspicious – I saw none of my silver. I saw no evidence of wealth at all, actually."

Emma's curiosity was diverted. "What are his lodgings like?"

"Small, cramped, but very neat. The man has two daughters, about twelve and eleven."

"Two daughters?"

"Why not? They are also small – rather dark-complexioned, like their father – and their names are Florica and Kizzy."

"Really!" said Emma, rubbing her nose. "Did you speak to them?"

"I asked them – in front of their father and Mr. and Mrs. Gilbert – if either of them had seen anything suspicious."

"Two sharp-eyed girls might very well have seen something. And?"

"They told me nothing. Of course, they may have not felt comfortable talking to me. I have asked Mrs. Gilbert to chat with them later and tell me if they tell her anything."

Emma glanced at her needlework basket but did not pick it up; the theft was far more fascinating than embroidery. It seemed to her that the Draper fellow was still the most likely suspect. "What if Draper wanted to inspect your estate for opportunity and arranged for the bull to enter your turnip field?"

Mr. Knightley scratched his chin. "Perhaps. Gilbert *was* surprised that the animal went to my house. But it seems an inconvenient and unreliable way to go about it."

"Did Mr. Gilbert not tell you that Draper is a magician with animals?" asked Emma, pleased with herself at remembering this detail which supported her theory.

"Indeed, he did," said Mr. Knightley.

They sat together for a while without speaking. "What will you do?" asked Emma.

He had told William Larkins to fix the door, and to make it more secure, although it was rather like closing a stable door after the horse had bolted.

"Is there anything I can do?" Emma asked. "Go to Donwell and take a look?"

"Dear Emma, you cannot track down thieves!"

"I could look over the damage myself. I am your wife and Donwell Abbey will be my home someday." She was actually curious to look at the door and the area where the silver had been and to see if she could come up with any ideas.

"Emma, you are no expert in how thieves break into houses."

"Don't you value my opinion?" Emma asked, a little stung.

"Yes, but I really don't think there is anything significant to see, and if you come with me to Donwell Abbey you would only worry your father. Of course, the next time you come I can show you where everything happened. However, I will prove to you that I value your opinion, for there is a matter on which I want consult you: how shall we break this to John and to Isabella?"

Emma considered. Mr. John Knightley's temper was much more volatile than his older brother's, whereas her sister Isabella was almost as nervous as Mr. Woodhouse, having inherited their father's disposition. So John would be angry about the injury to his boyhood home, and Isabella would be terrified for everyone in the vicinity of Highbury.

"I don't see what we can do but write to them and to let them know what happened," said Emma. "*You* had better write to your brother, for you can describe what has been stolen better than I."

"They will be horrified that crime has come to Highbury," said Mr. Knightley.

"Indeed. And how many homes are broken into in London – how many pockets are picked in the city, even in Brunswick Square?" asked Emma.

That brought a smile to her husband's lips. "You are right," he said, "and you remind me, too, that far worse things have happened. But I advise you not to use this argument in front of your father; he will only grow anxious for Isabella and the children."

"You can rely on my discretion."

"And I promise you that you can rely on mine," said Mr. Knightley. "I am sorry I upset him this morning."

"No, no, you could not help saying what you did. And how could this event be kept from him? I thank you for sending Mr. Weston here, especially when you were so very worried and very busy. Now, about informing our relations in Brunswick Square?"

"Very well, I will write a short note to John about the event, and you can write the details to your sister."

"But I have not seen them myself! Oh! Don't worry – I know you are very busy. We will have years and years to spend at Donwell Abbey, and then I can complain about not knowing what is going on in Hartfield. Perhaps Serle and James will run off to Scotland together and take my father's silver with them to finance their new existence."

At the prospect of Hartfield's weathered coachman and stout cook eloping, Mr. Knightley broke into a deep guffaw, and Emma felt she had banished his worries, at least for the night.

"I thought you had given up matchmaking," he teased.

"It is only a notion," she defended herself. "Serle and James have every opportunity – and certainly the maturity – to manage their own romance, if they have any inclination. But how well they could work together, if they wished! Serle knows where all the silver is – including the items we have not used since my mother died – and James is well-equipped to manage their escape."

"Nonsensical girl!" exclaimed Mr. Knightley, and pulled her close.

Emma leaned against his shoulder. She was glad to make him laugh and to help him relax but she wanted her husband to respect her opinions, too. Then her mind wandered back to Serle and James: it was amazing how easily nonsense could be arranged to sound like sense. And why should not the cook and the coachman have a romantic attachment if they wished? True, they were neither young nor attractive, nor educated nor rich, but no one had a monopoly on love.

11 CALLING ON MRS. CHURCHILL

Two days after the theft was discovered at Donwell Abbey, Mr. Woodhouse's spirits had recovered sufficiently for Emma to venture beyond the shrubbery of Hartfield. Mr. Knightley reminded her that she should call on Mrs. Churchill, so in the afternoon she walked to Highbury. It was so pleasant outside – the sun bright but not strong – that she thought that there was a good chance that Miss Bates and Mrs. Churchill would not be at home. Probably they were out, calling on the Westons, or the Coles, or even on the Eltons. In that case she would leave a message with the servant and feel as if she had done her duty without being punished.

Visiting Miss Bates had always been a penance for Emma; the garrulous spinster might be everything worthy and good, yet Emma's patience was tried by her. What would Miss Bates do with herself, she wondered, as she walked briskly along the road. Well, if the ladies were at home, she could inquire. Perhaps she would go to live with her niece and then Emma would be spared the pricks of conscience that Miss Bates always provoked. But although Emma could control her behavior – and she resolved to listen to Miss Bates, no matter what she said, for the poor woman still had to be mourning the loss of her mother – how could she regulate her feelings? How could she make herself like someone when she did not?

She stopped first at Ford's and ordered a *pair* of jugs to be delivered to Mrs. Robert Martin. If Harriet dropped one, she would still have a spare.

"Very good, Mrs. Knightley," said Mrs. Ford.

"I heard you have some new blue silk?" Emma asked.

"We did, but Mrs. Elton purchased it just this morning."

"Oh!"

"Shall I let you know if we receive another fine silk, Madam?"

"Yes, thank you," said Emma. She said good-bye to Mrs. Ford and crossed the street, thinking that the Eltons could not be suffering financially if Mrs. Elton was ordering fine silk. Perhaps she had guessed incorrectly about their situation – or perhaps Churchills *had* made a substantial donation in the memory of Jane's grandmother.

Emma entered the building in which Miss Bates lived and climbed the dark, narrow stairs. She was a little disappointed as Miss Bates's words gushed down the stairs, and downright annoyed as they were followed by the sharp tones of Mrs. Elton. Penance indeed! Extremely severe! And with Miss Bates and Mrs. Elton in the apartment, any attempt on her part to improve her acquaintance with Mrs. Churchill would be thwarted.

Emma paused on the stairs, considering turning around and running away. She could manage it easily, for the staircase, despite being dark and narrow, did not creak. But what would she tell Mr. Knightley? Nay, that would not do. And if Miss Bates and Mrs. Elton spared her from having to become an intimate of Mrs. Churchill, then at least they were good for something.

What was wrong with her, Emma wondered, that she disliked so many people? As expiation she continued up the stairs and knocked at Miss Bates's apartment door.

"Mrs. Knightley! How good of you to come!" Miss Bates's welcome was so effusive, so warm and so genuine, that Emma could not help feeling ashamed – as she had so many times before – to think that she had hesitated to make this visit. Even Mrs. Churchill greeted her with a smile as well and invited her to sit in the chair beside hers. Only Mrs. Elton's hello was grudging.

After the usual pleasantries were exchanged, and inquiries made and answered about their mutual health – all claiming that they and their families were fine, although privately Emma thought that Mrs. Churchill looked pale and fatigued – Emma inquired discreetly about Miss Bates's spirits.

"So kind of you to ask, Mrs. Knightley – can't believe that Mother left us such a short while ago—" she wiped away a tear, and smiled, "-and yet life moves on. I have scarcely had a moment alone, thanks to visits from kind friends such as Mrs. Elton, the Coles and the Westons, and especially dear Jane, who has been kind enough to stay and has been helping me sort through my mother's papers. I had no idea how much my mother wrote – how accomplished and clever she was – you can see where our dear Jane's brains came from! She was quite the artist, too."

"How interesting," said Emma. "And you are wearing your mother's locket."

"Yes, I am. It still feels strange, to consider it mine, but it does make me feel close to her."

"But we have been discussing something else," Mrs. Elton objected.

"Yes, of course we have, something much more important and immediate and exciting than my mother's old papers and her gold locket. Mrs. Elton has arranged something that sounds wonderful – so exciting for Highbury – what do you call it? – a musical afternoon at the Vicarage."

"I think I heard you mention it at…" Emma, began, but as she recalled the discussion had been at the Crown Inn, just after Mrs. Bates's burial, she did not continue.

"Just so," said Mrs. Elton, talking over Emma's words, either because she wanted to spare Miss Bates from being reminded of her mother's funeral or because she preferred the sound of her voice to Mrs. Knightley's. "There is talent in this parish – unrecognized talent – and I intend to do what I can to make sure that these young voices are heard. So on an afternoon a few days from now, at the Vicarage I will have a musical afternoon for them."

Emma was curious despite herself. "Which young voices have you found to exhibit?"

Mrs. Elton mentioned several names – a few students from Mrs. Goddard's boarding-school, a young shepherd who worked for the Martins – and then Florica and Kizzy Draper.

"Florica and Kizzy!" Emma exclaimed, surprised to hear these names again so soon.

"Hardly Christian names, I know," explained Mrs. Elton, misinterpreting Emma's reaction, "but at least their father's name, Noah, is respectable. And Mr. E. did not christen them – nor did any vicar of Highbury, as they are wandering folk. But the girls sing pretty duets, and what if we could offer them something better?"

"Indeed," said Mrs. Churchill, "the hope of something better is important for young people. Even if those hopes never come to fruition."

Emma glanced briefly at Jane, and wondered what reason that young matron had to sound so bleak. Mrs. Churchill was rich, talented and elegant; her husband doted on her. Perhaps it was being back in Highbury, in this apartment, recalling the time when her own future had seemed so uncertain? When her best prospect had been to go out as a governess, taking care of other people's children, a life of servitude and degradation? Yet if staying in her childhood home brought forth those memories, then why remain in this apartment when she could stay at Randalls?

These thoughts raced through Emma, but she pushed them aside; Jane's grandmother had been dead only a short while, and perhaps Jane still mourned her. If Mrs. Bates had been as talented as Miss Bates claimed – and certainly Jane's brains must have come from somewhere – then perhaps she was thinking of her grandmother's life as a life wasted.

"Just so," Mrs. Elton agreed sycophantically with Mrs. Churchill, "children need hope. Now that Mr. E. has returned from London, we can finally select a day."

"Mr. Elton has already returned from London? I hope his business in the city was successful," Emma said.

"Quite successful," said Mrs. Elton. "He came back yesterday with the chest that belonged to his father – no accounting for taste, but it means a lot to my husband."

There was such a gleam in Mrs. Elton's eyes as she spoke that Emma was a little taken aback: how could a chest be so important? Perhaps it had a secret drawer that contained gold. Nay, she was being ridiculous; she struggled to repress her fancy.

"As I was saying, we can now choose a day and so I came here to confer with Miss Bates and Jane – I mean, Mrs. Churchill – to see if Thursday next suits them. It does, and it suits the Westons and the Coles. I hope you and Knightley can make it."

The last sentence was not uttered very graciously, and Emma noted that while the Coles, the Westons and Mrs. Churchill were consulted as to the time and day that best suited them, she and Mr. Knightley were pointedly not. Nevertheless, Emma was curious to see the Draper girls for herself, and curious, too, to take a look inside the Vicarage and see if she could detect any symptoms of penny-pinching. "I'm sure we will be delighted," said Emma.

Mrs. Elton did not look especially pleased, but of course she had to know it would be better for the local children if the Knightleys came to her musical afternoon rather than staying away, so her words were gracious although her manner was not.

Emma tried, during the remainder of her visit, to engage Mrs. Churchill in conversation, but Miss Bates and Mrs. Elton made it almost impossible – and Mrs. Churchill was little help. Emma asked Jane how long she expected to stay in Highbury – Jane did not know – she then invited Jane to call any time she liked at Hartfield – Jane thanked her for the offer of hospitality but gave no hint that she would partake of it. The only improvement that Emma detected in Jane's manner towards herself was that Jane, at least, did not seem angry or jealous. The best description was reserved, which might be simply be a defense to her aunt's loquaciousness and Mrs. Elton's affectation.

Miss Bates prattled on about many things, especially remembering how talented Jane had been as a child and how grateful they had been when she received opportunities, while Mrs. Elton made it clear that she would out-stay Mrs. Knightley and prevent her from having anything resembling a tête-à-tête with Mrs. Churchill. Defeated, but feeling that she had given her best, Emma said she needed to return to Hartfield. It really was time, so she wished the ladies well and departed. As she descended the dark and narrow staircase and re-emerged into Highbury's bright sunshine, she wondered if she and Mrs. Churchill would ever be friends – and if that young matron still had something to hide.

12 MRS. ELTON'S MUSICAL AFTERNOON

Time passed in Highbury. Mr. Knightley spent most of his days at Donwell Abbey, working on the harvest, while Mrs. Weston made brief morning visits to Hartfield with her daughter. Emma received a short note from Harriet Martin thanking her for the jugs. Letters arrived from Brunswick Square. Isabella was dreadfully shocked that such a terrible theft could occur so close to her childhood home, while Mr. John Knightley remarked that human nature was the same everywhere. The members of the parishes of Highbury and Donwell, all aware of the theft at Donwell Abbey, took care locking their doors and guarding their possessions. Either because the thief had departed or because the locals had become more cautious, no one reported any additional break-ins. Gradually the talk shifted from burglary to music, as the event at the Vicarage approached.

The great day arrived at last, and Mr. and Mrs. Knightley went to the Eltons for the afternoon concert, their carriage experiencing no difficulties despite Mr. Woodhouse's concern about the turn into Vicarage Lane. Emma had not been there in many months, and so her eyes were wide for signs of improvement and alterations.

"Knightley! Mrs. Knightley! You are the first to arrive. Mr. Woodhouse could not come, I take it? What a pity; the afternoon should be a real treat," said Mrs. Elton, and Emma saw that Mrs. Elton was wearing a new dress made of blue silk.

"Sam here will take your coats," said Mr. Elton, and Emma recognized Sam, one of the waiters at the Crown Inn, obviously hired for the afternoon. "Come this way, please."

"Our humble abode is nothing compared to Maple Grove – or even Hartfield – but I hope you will find it comfortable, at least for an afternoon."

They followed Mrs. Elton, who was all smiles, and indeed, the Vicarage looked lovely, although some of the furniture had been rearranged in the parlor for the concert, with space at one end for the piano and the performers, and chairs everywhere else for the audience. While Mr. Knightley spoke to Mr. Elton, Emma, without any qualms or hesitations, complimented Mrs. Elton on the excellence of her arrangements.

"It has been a while since you were here last," said Mrs. Elton, laughing a little. "We have both become mothers, of course, since then – babies do upset the household."

"They do indeed," Emma agreed. "Where is young Philip?"

"My nursemaid is taking care of him, as I imagine, your nursemaid is caring for your son."

"Yes, of course," said Emma. She spied an unfamiliar piece of furniture – a tall chest. "Is that what Mr. Elton brought back with him from London?"

"Yes, it is. Not much to look at, I know, but it belonged to his father. We all must humor our *caro sposos*, must we not?" and Mrs. Elton laughed affectedly. "Excuse me – sit anywhere you like – more guests are arriving."

And, dragging her husband along with her, even though he was in mid-sentence with Mr. Knightley, the Eltons returned to their front door, leaving the two Knightleys standing amidst the many chairs.

"Where shall we sit?" asked Mr. Knightley, and then, as he was tall and did not want to block the view of others, suggested they take seats a little out of the way, against the wall. It was not a place of honor – and excepting possibly Mrs. Churchill, the Knightleys would be "first" in this gathering – but Mr. Knightley then said, quoting Luke, "Go and sit down in the lowest place."

"I suppose we should honor Christian values in the Vicarage," Emma said, and agreed privately with Mrs. Elton that occasionally wives needed to humor their husbands. They sat beside the chest that Mr. Elton had just brought back from London, which gave Emma plenty of time to examine it.

"And, what do you think?" Mr. Knightley whispered. "Are the Eltons about to be carted off to the poor house?"

"It does not look like it," Emma conceded, observing the little touches of elegance scattered around the room, from the polished silver on the sideboard, evidence of the refreshment that would be served afterwards, to the lace trimming Mrs. Elton's new gown. "The only odd note is this chest."

"That is here for sentimental reasons," said Mr. Knightley.

"Even if Mr. Elton is particularly fond of it, why does Mrs. Elton permit it in her parlor? Why is it not in Mr. Elton's study, where he can enjoy it without its being an eyesore to everyone else?"

"Perhaps Mr. Elton insisted."

"Perhaps," said Emma dubiously, studying the item of furniture in question and wondering how something so plain could matter so much to Mr. Elton. "Perhaps it is a chest with a secret drawer and a map to treasure," she whispered.

Mr. Knightley laughed, and then added, "If so, why would they put it in the parlor?"

Emma could not understand it, but her speculations were interrupted by the entrance of others. The Westons and the Coles greeted them. Mrs. Weston, who adored music, was especially looking forward to it, her face pink with anticipation.

"Why are you sitting *here*, Mrs. Knightley?" asked Mrs. Cole. "Hidden away in a corner?"

"The fault is mine," said Mr. Knightley. "I did not want to block others' view."

"Very thoughtful of you, Knightley," said Mr. Cole, choosing another out-of-the-way spot. "And very enterprising of Mrs. Elton to organize this."

"I understand that there are nearly a dozen performers," said Mrs. Weston, as she and her husband sat beside the Knightleys.

Despite herself, Emma was impressed. "How did Mrs. Elton find them all?"

"She asked Mr. Elton," said Mrs. Cole. "As the vicar, Mr. Elton travels around the parish and even beyond. She asked him some time ago to listen for budding musicians."

Emma was even more impressed. "She has been planning this for a while, then."

"She has been hoping to," said Mrs. Cole. "She discussed it with me a while ago but put it off – the birth of little Philip – but just recently, she decided to move ahead."

"We're looking forward to it," said Mr. Weston, but yawned – he was not nearly as musical as his wife.

At that point more of the best of Highbury entered, Mr. and Mrs. Perry, the Coxes and Mrs. Goddard, filling up the room. Soon Emma thought they would have to start; the air was growing stuffy. Then someone opened a window, and she suffered a draught.

"It is just as well that your father did not come," said Mr. Knightley, helping her adjust her shawl.

"Yes," said Emma, for it was crowded and the noise level was rising. "He would not have done well."

"I wonder why we are waiting?" murmured Mr. Knightley.

"Perhaps some difficulty with a performer," suggested Mrs. Weston. "So many young people…"

They *were* waiting for someone particular; the matter became clear when Miss Bates entered the room. "Mrs. Elton, I am so sorry to be late – not usually tardy – but Jane was not feeling well, and finally I convinced her to lie down."

"You mean to say that Jane – I mean, Mrs. Churchill – is not coming?" Mrs. Elton's voice rose with anger and disappointment, so much so that everyone else halted their conversations in order to look at Miss Bates and Mrs. Elton.

Emma repressed a smile.

Mr. Elton covered for his wife. "I'm sorry your niece is not well, Miss Bates. I hope it is nothing serious."

"I hope not, too. I offered to stay with her, but Jane insisted that I come. She said if she could only lie down a little while and sleep she would do better. I did not like how she looked. But she tells me she is well, only exhausted."

"What on earth has she to exhaust her?" asked Mrs. Elton, who was clearly put out by not being able to impress her great friend, the wealthy Mrs. Churchill.

Emma wondered too. Was Mrs. Churchill truly unwell; was she unwilling to spend time with Mrs. Elton; or was there some other reason she wished to be alone in her aunt's apartment?

"Augusta, others are waiting to hear the performers," said Mr. Elton, who was more concerned with keeping his parishioners happy than currying the favor of one rich lady who usually lived far away.

Miss Bates, fingering the gold locket at her neck, apologized again for the absence of her niece. "Mrs. Elton, Jane is so disappointed – wishes she could come – she wishes you a great success today – I can't wait to get home to describe it to her."

Mrs. Elton frowned until another prompting from her husband forced her to resume her role as hostess. Miss Bates was assisted by Mr. Elton – still apologizing for her niece's absence, Mr. Elton found her a seat – and Mrs. Elton went to the front of the room and called everyone to order. "Good afternoon," she said and then began a speech that she had obviously rehearsed a few times beforehand, welcoming them to the Vicarage and hoping that they would enjoy listening to some of Highbury's native talent.

Mrs. Elton finished her introductory remarks and then the first song, sung by a student from Mrs. Goddard's school, accompanied by another on Mrs. Elton's piano – just tuned for the occasion – was pleasant enough. Everyone applauded, and the young singer, red-faced and breathless, sat down on a bench in the back of the room. The pianist then played another piece. Several more young musicians performed: a flute-player, a few more singers and a fellow on a violin, and finally the gypsy pair – Miss Florica and Miss Kizzy Draper – from the Gilbert farm. They were slender, small, and rather dark complexioned, but their black eyes gleamed with intelligence. Curious, Emma leaned forward.

The two Draper girls sang very well, so well, in fact, that Mrs. Elton's audience was loath for their performance to end. Someone asked for an encore; others took up the call, and Mrs. Elton told them to sing another song.

The girls consulted with each other and then began again, a lively piece about selling fish. They sang it well, but Mrs. Weston raised her eyebrows and Mr. Weston and Mr. Knightley looked as if they were about to burst out laughing. Emma wanted to ask what the matter was, but did not want to speak while the girls were singing – and then she heard the ribald nature of the lyrics. Mrs. Elton flushed and then Mr. Elton jumped up.

"That will be enough – thank you, that will be enough," said the vicar.

The girls stopped; Mr. Elton called for applause while Mrs. Elton ushered the Draper girls away. Mr. Elton then invited everyone to stay for tea and cakes. Chairs were moved by a couple of servants; the young performers and Mrs. Elton were congratulated, and the vicar's wife recovered a little from the momentary embarrassment.

"Yes, well, I have long meant to arrange a musical afternoon here in Highbury. I am the patroness of the musicians, you see, although on a very small scale, but I hope the scale is at least in tune!" laughing affectedly.

Her listeners assured her that all was in order, in fact that all was excellent, and Mrs. Elton was evidently so pleased with her phrasing that she used it in many conversations. Emma complimented Mrs. Elton for all her arrangements, from the food, tea and wine, and for introducing a novelty into Highbury. Then she moved to Miss Bates and inquired after Mrs. Churchill's health.

"You are so very kind," said Miss Bates. "She is just tired, inexplicably tired. I can't understand it. In every other respect she is well, but she wishes to retire early and yet she sleeps so long!"

Mr. Knightley asked if Mr. Perry had been consulted.

"No, Jane refuses to see him; she says it is nothing and that she will be well soon. She even forbade me to mention her fatigue to him, which is unfortunate, because I can't seem to help talking about it, and Mr. Perry will hear me, and he will be so concerned. Of course, expense is not an issue, but she still insists. Mr. and Mrs. Knightley, if you do not help me control my tongue, I will certainly let it drop, and then Jane will be so angry! But I cannot help myself, it seems – oh, this cheese is excellent."

"If you like, we can offer you a ride back to Highbury in the carriage," said Emma, thinking that the best way to keep Miss Bates from revealing Jane's fatigue to anyone else would be simply to remove her altogether.

"Ah! You are so kind! But it is a pleasant day, my shoes are comfortable, and as long as I am here I wish to visit my mother's grave, as it is on the way."

"Of course," said Emma, feeling that she had done her duty to guard Jane's privacy – she was no magician; she could not prevent Miss Bates's gush of words – and then Miss Bates's attention was captured by Mr. Weston.

"Miss Bates, how is Jane?" asked Mr. Weston, naturally concerned about the health of his daughter-in-law.

As Miss Bates began repeating again what she had told her niece she would not repeat, Emma moved aside so that she was standing next to Mrs. Weston. Emma spoke with self-command about the excellence of Mrs. Elton's afternoon.

"The music was lovely," said Mrs. Weston. "Especially that young shepherd and those last two girls – although they obviously need some more advice on which songs they should sing. Perhaps we should have more afternoons like this. Of course it is not like a concert in London or even in Kingston, but it is very pleasant."

"Yes," Emma said. "We should not be too nice. And Mrs. Elton has put an effort into making this an agreeable afternoon. Perhaps we should do these entertainments more frequently, but I am afraid that Mrs. Elton has already located all the talent in the parish." She then saw something which puzzled her.

"What is it, Emma?" asked Mrs. Weston, who as she had raised Emma since she was a little girl, knew every expression of her former charge's countenance.

Emma immediately smoothed the confusion from her face. "Nothing, my dear friend. Nothing – I was mistaken. But I am a little concerned about the time. My father will start to worry, and I have been away from the baby too long. Please excuse me." As they had been gone rather long, she pushed through the crowd to her husband; he agreed they should leave and sent a servant to alert their coachman James. Once more they offered a ride home to Miss Bates; once more the middle-aged spinster refused with thanks and many more thanks. Then they made their farewells to the Eltons, explaining that they had to get home to the baby.

"Of course, your Georgie is younger than my Philip," said Mrs. Elton. Mrs. Knightley might be richer and claim a better ancestry than Mrs. Elton and thus have a higher rank in Highbury, but Mrs. Elton's child was a few months older than Emma's, and she used those months as a reason to dispense advice whenever they met. "Can your boy sit up yet?"

"I will go home and see," Emma said.

The Knightleys learned that their carriage was ready. A servant helped them with their coats, and they went outside. Mr. Knightley assisted Emma into the carriage, then stepped in after her. Mr. Knightley tapped the ceiling of the carriage, and the staid horses from the Woodhouse stable started their usual walk under James' careful direction.

After the carriage had turned into the road, Mr. Knightley teased his wife: "What did you think?"

"It was both pleasant and original," said Emma.

"And do you still think the Eltons are suffering financial distress?"

"I saw no sign of it," Emma admitted, as they rolled past the church and the cemetery beside it. "But that chest was very odd, don't you think?"

"What more do you have to say about Mr. Elton's chest?"

"Did you not see that Mr. Elton placed his glass on it? It could make a ring."

"And?"

"If he is so attached to a piece of furniture that he traveled to London to bring it back – if he values it so much – then why would he risk damaging it?"

"My dear, I cannot explain it, but I confess I have little curiosity as well. I try to be interested in your concerns, but the vicar's treatment of an old piece of furniture is just not worth pursuing."

Emma fell silent. Mr. Knightley, she knew, was a little cross. He had work to do at Donwell Abbey but he had sacrificed his afternoon for this event.

"Perhaps we should not worry so much about our neighbors," said Mr. Knightley, "and let them place their chests and their crockery where they wish. It is, after all, their house; not really your concern and not an issue worthy of your fertile imagination."

"You are right, it *is* trivial," Emma conceded.

"I am sure that something more interesting will occur to divert you," Mr. Knightley said, as if he was a little ashamed of his brief display of bad temper. "What about Jane Churchill's not coming to Mrs. Elton's? Is she just tired, or is there another reason that she chooses to slight Mrs. Elton? Mrs. Elton was not pleased."

"No, but with respect to Jane Churchill I refuse to speculate," Emma said, although she had suspicions. "I speculated too much the last time she stayed in Highbury."

"I appreciate your desire for discretion," said Mr. Knightley, with approval, as the carriage turned into the Hartfield drive. He opened the door and helped her out.

"As you say, something more interesting will occur to occupy me."

13 MRS. CHURCHILL COMES TO HARTFIELD

The Knightleys were right in believing that something would happen, although they would never have predicted the event that would provide a topic of horrified conversation for all of the inhabitants of Highbury for the next days and weeks. The Knightleys were the first to learn that something was wrong. After dinner on the day of the musical afternoon, when they were sitting in the parlor before the fire and Mr. Woodhouse was yawning and talking about a basin of gruel before going to bed, there was a knock at the door. They all looked at each other with surprise. "Who could it be?" Emma asked blankly.

"William Larkins?" Mr. Knightley wondered aloud, bouncing his son on his knee.

Mr. Woodhouse said nothing but blinked with alarm.

The suspense regarding the identity of the nighttime caller did not last long; the butler ushered in Jane Churchill. Her face was pale, as if she was ill.

"Mrs. Churchill?" they all asked in surprise.

"My dear young lady, whatever are you doing here?" queried Mr. Woodhouse, concerned astonishment causing him to speak with unusual bluntness.

"Please, come in," said Emma, rising and guiding Jane to a comfortable chair near the fireplace, and helping her to sit down.

"My apologies for disturbing you at such an hour, Mr. Woodhouse, Mrs. Knightley – but I need assistance – Mr. Knightley's assistance," said Jane Churchill.

"Yes, of course, what can I do for you?" asked Mr. Knightley.

"My aunt has not returned from the musical afternoon at the Eltons."

"What?" asked Emma, glancing at the clock. "But that ended hours ago."

"Could she have stayed for supper?" inquired Mr. Knightley. "Have you checked with the Eltons?"

"Not yet," said Mrs. Churchill.

"No? It seems like the first thing to do," said Mr. Knightley.

Emma and her husband exchanged a look, and Emma wondered if Jane really did have a problem with the Eltons. "The Eltons live further away from Mrs. Churchill," Emma offered. "As do the Westons. If she is fatigued, then it is natural for her to come first to Hartfield."

Mr. Knightley said nothing, but his look indicated to Emma that he did not believe her excuse for Jane, but that he would not dispute it or discuss it – at least not now, not until they had a chance to speak in private.

"I know the Eltons must be consulted, but it seems unlikely that my aunt is with them. My aunt knew I was fatigued, and she would never have stayed longer than she promised. I am sorry for disturbing you, Mr. Knightley, but I feel that you are the person I can most rely on in this matter."

"Of course, I am happy to be of assistance. Do you have any objection to my consulting the Eltons? Or the Westons?"

Mrs. Churchill bit her lip. "I suppose not, Mr. Knightley. They will have to know anyway."

Mr. Knightley spoke briefly with Emma, handing her the baby and telling her to take care of Jane, and explaining that he would first head to the Eltons to learn anything if he could. He put on his coat and hat, wrapped a scarf around his neck, and departed into the chilly night.

"Mrs. Churchill, are you hungry? Can we get you some tea? Or anything more?"

"I am a little hungry," Jane admitted.

"Would you like a basin of gruel?" asked Mr. Woodhouse. "Or we can arrange to have an egg boiled, if it would please you – our dear Serle knows how to boil an egg."

"Some bread and butter, if you have it, and tea," answered Jane.

Emma rang the bell, ordered refreshment for her guest and gruel for her father, and asked the nursery-maid to take the baby and to put him to bed, while wondering what they should talk about. Jane's health seemed out of the question, and it seemed just as indiscreet to inquire about her reluctance to be with the Eltons – and the Westons? Of course, Hartfield *was* closest, and if Jane was fatigued, why not come here? Mr. Knightley was the most capable man she knew. *She* thought that, and Harriet Martin thought that – why would not Jane Churchill think that?

"I do hope my old friend Miss Bates is all right," Mr. Woodhouse said anxiously. "Neither of you should be wandering around after dark. Not after what happened at Donwell Abbey."

"Papa, there is no need to alarm Mrs. Churchill," said Emma.

"I am trying not to be alarmed," confessed Jane. "Trying, but not succeeding."

"But what could happen to her?" asked Emma. "Unless she twisted her ankle walking in the dark? Yet tonight the moon is nearly full; Miss Bates should have no problem seeing where she is going."

"Perhaps my aunt did twist an ankle," said Jane, and this idea seemed to offer her so much relief that Emma's stomach lurched. What was Mrs. Churchill imagining?

Fortunately the food arrived, sparing Emma the need to find a subject. She busied herself with pouring tea and making a plate for Jane, and Mr. Woodhouse again pressed their visitor to consider a small basin of gruel. Jane pleased the gentle old man by accepting his offer, and soon they were discussing the merits of gruel and how few seemed to understand the importance of a smooth consistency, not too thin, not too thick. Once Emma caught Jane's eye, and read alarm there, but Mrs. Churchill, biting her lip, quickly looked away.

Whatever the matter was, they would find out soon, thought Emma. The clock struck nine, and Mr. Knightley had not yet returned. Mr. Woodhouse yawned.

"Mrs. Churchill, if you will excuse me, I will retire."

"Of course," said Jane.

"I am an old man, regular in my habits. Besides, my daughter Emma will be happy to keep you company. I cannot wish you a better companion than Emma."

"Do not remain up on my account, Mr. Woodhouse. Mrs. Knightley and I will do very well together."

Assisted by a servant, Mr. Woodhouse made his slow way out of the room, leaving Emma alone with Jane.

"I am all too aware of how much trouble I am causing you, Mrs. Knightley," Jane apologized. "If you wish to retire as well, I am sure I will be all right."

"I am not tired," Emma said, "but I suspect that you are. Would you like to sleep yourself? We can have a bedroom made ready in a few minutes."

Jane shook her head. "No, thank you."

"I sense something serious is bothering you," said Emma after a while. "If you would care to talk about it, I am ready to listen. You can rely on my discretion. If you prefer to remain silent, I will respect that too."

Jane answered slowly. "I thank you, Mrs. Knightley, and I know that my reserve in the past has been unattractive to many – I expect including you."

"I never had the right—"

"Ah, but you did, did you not? The way Frank flirted with you was difficult for me, of course, but what if *you* had fallen in love with him? Then you would have suffered, and have suffered innocently, whereas I at least knew what was going on. And although I was angry with him, I was also angry with you, which was wrong of me."

"Mrs. Churchill, there is no need," said Emma. Although Mr. Knightley wanted her to find a friend in Jane Churchill – and what a surprise that it should be happening *this* way – she did not really want to revisit the mistakes and misunderstandings of several years ago. "My own behavior was inexcusable. I was not attached to Mr. Churchill, so why was I flirting with him? Let us not worry about the past."

"It is easier to talk about the past than it is for me to discuss the present," said Jane, with half a smile. "I know you must be wondering why, after apologizing for being reserved more than a year ago, I continue to maintain my reserve now. But, Mrs. Knightley, my fears – my hopes – are not mine to reveal; what I suspect would do harm if repeated."

"I will not press you," Emma said, and they both fell silent. Jane closed her eyes and leaned her head back against the chair, but although Emma was silent, her mind worked busily. What on earth did Jane suspect? She felt as if she had been given a set of scrambled letters and was trying to form them into words, into a complete phrase, but her combinations, her rearrangements, made no sense. Was Jane in Highbury just to comfort her aunt or was there some other reason for her being here? Why did Jane not go to either the Westons or the Eltons? And that chest of Mr. Elton's – was he really so fond of it?

She had many questions but no answers. All she could see was that Jane was staying with her aunt during a sad time in that person's life, and if the apartment in Highbury was not the most comfortable, well, it was Jane's childhood home, and she was accustomed to its privations. Besides, the money she had now probably alleviated those privations considerably. As for the Eltons' affection towards old furniture, it might be peculiar, but she was at a loss to find an explanation for it of any significance.

Despite Jane's avowal that she would not spend the night at Hartfield, Emma stepped into the hall and told a servant to prepare a bedroom for her, so the servants themselves could retire if they wished to. As the maid went off to fulfill her orders, the door opened and Mr. Knightley entered.

Even in the dim light of the hall, Emma could see that her husband was upset. "What is it?" she asked, helping him off with his hat and coat.

He squeezed her hand with cold fingers. "Where is Jane?"

"In the parlor," Emma said. "What is it?"

He lowered his voice. "Miss Bates is dead."

14 DEATH OF A SPINSTER

"No!" Emma cried. "What happened?"

"I will tell you all I know. Fetch the brandy and then join me in the parlor."

Emma went to the dining room, and hastily prepared a tray with the brandy and three glasses, then joined her husband and their guest in the parlor. Mr. Knightley had pulled up a footstool and had seated himself on it, while Jane blinked sleepily, and then with alarm at the expressions on her hosts' faces.

"What is it? Tell me – tell me at once," she implored.

"You were right to be worried," he said gently. "Miss Bates was found – dead – lying on top of the graves of your grandparents."

Emma quickly poured a glass of brandy and passed it to Jane, then poured two more, one for her husband and another for herself. "Drink this – please. Mr. Knightley, is it certain? Has Mr. Perry been called?"

"Mr. Perry has been called, but I am afraid it is certain," Mr. Knightley said. "Your aunt was certainly not breathing, and she was as cold as the earth beneath her."

"Can you tell me anything more?" asked Jane. "Is anything known about how she died?"

"Jane – Mrs. Churchill – I think it would be better if you first got a full night's sleep, and we discussed the details when we know more, in the light of day."

"I have had a room prepared," Emma said. "I know you said you would rather go home, but in the circumstances—"

Jane glanced briefly at Emma, nodded, and then turned back to Mr. Knightley. "You know something more," she said. "I want to know what it is."

Mr. Knightley sipped his brandy, then spoke slowly. "Very well. You have a right to know. Miss Bates's head was bashed in."

Jane closed her eyes and slumped in her seat, while Emma was stunned. "I don't understand," Emma asked. "Did that happen when she fell? Or—" and the horror sank in.

"She was killed by someone," Mr. Knightley said bluntly.

Emma shivered. "That is terrible," she whispered. "Absolutely terrible."

"Do you know anything more? What has happened with – her body?" asked Jane.

"Mr. Perry is taking your aunt's body to the undertaker," said Mr. Knightley. "I have asked him to come here later, partly because I was afraid you might need his services. Miss Bates told us you were not feeling well, and this cannot help."

"I am not ill," Jane assured them, and sighed.

"What more can you tell us, Mr. Knightley?" asked Emma. "What did you do?"

Mr. Knightley asked that more tea be prepared – it would be a long night – and then he settled back to give them all the details of his evening. He had gone first, naturally, to the Eltons – but they explained that Miss Bates had left hours ago – certainly in sufficient time to reach home before dark.

Mr. Elton had volunteered to accompany him in the search for Miss Bates, and Mr. Knightley accepted the offer. Mr. Knightley suggested that they walk from the Vicarage towards the town, and then recalled that Miss Bates had said something about stopping at the cemetery to visit the graves of her parents. "Yes," Mr. Elton agreed, "she wanted to see that her mother's grave was in order."

So they walked slowly in the dark, calling Miss Bates's name aloud, and looking carefully for any sign of a woman in distress.

But when they entered the cemetery, they found her body at once. She was lying, as Mr. Knightley had already said, across her parents' graves. Mr. Knightley had knelt down, turned her over, and determined that she was deceased – but he sent Mr. Elton to fetch Mr. Perry anyway. Although Mr. Elton had seen dead bodies before, he was nevertheless shaken by the discovery. Mr. Knightley felt it was better to give the vicar something to do.

"But were you not frightened?" asked Emma, alarmed for her husband. "A killer was about!"

"There is a difference in attacking me, and poor Miss Bates," said Mr. Knightley. "I am not a likely victim. Besides, the churchyard was empty - and I was on my guard."

"What more can you tell us?" asked Jane.

While Mr. Elton went to fetch assistance, Mr. Knightley, waiting with Miss Bates's dead body, had had time to look around. The brightness of the moonlight made discovery possible. He found a rock, part of a broken old gravestone – heavy but not too heavy for a strong arm to wield – it looked to have blood on it. He thought it was what had been used to kill Miss Bates.

Jane looked ill as he described this; Emma reached out and squeezed her hand. Jane squeezed Emma's hand in return, but then released it and sat up straight, as if resolved to bear her burdens alone. "What more do you know – or suspect, Mr. Knightley?" she persisted.

There was the matter of the locket; the gold locket that had once belonged to Mrs. Bates. As far as Mr. Knightley could tell, it was missing. He thought that it had been on her neck that afternoon; was he correct?

"I remember seeing it," said Emma.

"Yes, she put it on before she left," Jane said. "So – do you think this was *robbery*?" she asked, a little incredulous.

"I am just telling you that I did not see it. I searched the area, but not very thoroughly, as it was dark. Perhaps it fell off between the Eltons' and the churchyard, or perhaps it is in her reticule. Here it is," he said, pulling it out of his pocket and holding it out to Jane. "I did not feel right, opening it."

Jane took her aunt's reticule and opened it and shook the contents out on the table beside her. They all leaned forward, scanning for the locket, but Miss Bates's belongings consisted of a few pence, a handkerchief, an old pencil and a small wad of court plaister. "I don't see it," she said.

"I examined your aunt's neck – it looked as if it was yanked off of her," said Mr. Knightley. "Was the locket very valuable?"

"It was gold," Jane said.

"So, it could be robbery," said Emma. "After all, Mr. Knightley, someone stole all your silver from Donwell Abbey."

"There is a difference, my dear Emma, between slipping into a mostly vacant estate to steal silver and murdering a woman in the village graveyard."

"Perhaps the thief at Donwell would have used violence if he had been discovered," said Emma, reaching out to pat his shoulder. "I am glad you were not there."

"And that Hodges did not happen upon him."

Emma looked at Jane, who was clutching her aunt's reticule like a talisman.

"It *is* more comforting to think my aunt might have been killed by a stranger as opposed to someone she knew," said Jane. "The first is terrible, but the latter is worse."

"Do you think it could have been someone she knew?" asked Mr. Knightley, but before Jane could answer that question, there was another bustle at the front door. Mr. Perry had arrived.

Emma poured tea, Mr. Knightley tossed another log on the fire, and Mr. Perry was invited to sit down. He told them that Miss Bates was definitely dead and that she must have died quickly from the blow. He informed Jane that he would send the body to the undertaker in the morning. He offered them all a sleeping draught, insisting especially that Jane take it.

"I should go home," said Jane, accepting the glass with Mr. Perry's medicine.

"Nonsense," said Emma. "How can you think it?"

"I cannot allow you to leave us," Mr. Knightley said. "Not under these circumstances."

"Come, let me take you upstairs," said Emma, and she helped Mrs. Churchill rise to her feet. "We are about the same size; you can wear one of my nightdresses."

They went upstairs, and Emma's maid, who had understood what was going on – if there was any night when the servants might be listening at the door, this was it, and it would save explanations later – and had laid out one of Emma's nightdresses and a nightcap. The lamp was lit, the bedding was fluffed and had been warmed with a warming pan; the water jug filled, and a towel placed out for the visitor's use. Emma left Mrs. Churchill alone to be assisted by her own maid – she checked on the baby in the meantime – and then came back when Jane was in bed.

"Is there anything you need?" Emma asked. "Are you comfortable enough?"

"No, thank you," said Jane. "I am grateful to you for your assistance." A tear slipped down her face.

Emma took a handkerchief from a chest of drawers and gave it to Jane. "I am so sorry about Miss Bates."

"It's my fault," Jane said, dabbing her eyes.

"Nonsense; how could it be your fault?"

"I should have gone with her," Jane said.

"Then you might have been killed as well," said Emma.

"I should have let her stay home, as she offered. I was tired, though, and I desired an afternoon to myself."

Miss Bates had been the kindest of women, but Emma had always thought that to be around the garrulous spinster without reprieve would be exhausting. "Do not blame yourself," Emma said, and again urged Jane to sleep. Jane thanked her again, closed her eyes, and Emma extinguished the candles.

15 THE DAY AFTER THE MURDER

Thanks to the Eltons, the Perrys and all the servants in their households and at Hartfield, the news of Miss Bates's murder spread throughout Highbury and the surrounding area with the rapidity of wind. Everyone was terribly shocked, especially Mr. Woodhouse, who became acquainted with the distressing news at his own breakfast table. It was dreadful, so beyond anything he had ever imagined – such things might happen in foreign parts and the worst neighborhoods of London – but never in Highbury, not his beloved, sweet, placid little Highbury. He trembled with fear in his chair, and frequently glanced with trepidation at the poker by the dining-room fireplace, as if alternately planning to use it as a weapon in his defense or fearing it might rise up and attack him.

Mrs. Jane Churchill, either due to staying up so late the night before, or from the sleeping draught Perry had administered, or from whatever condition was fatiguing her, was the last to descend. Her face was white and her eyes red and puffy.

Mr. Knightley helped her to a seat and Emma poured her some tea and inquired after Jane's health.

"I am still horrified and shocked," she said, "but other than that I am well, I thank you." She apologized for intruding on them and bringing such a disturbance into their home, with a gesture at Mr. Woodhouse's distress.

"It is not your fault," Emma said in a low voice – her father's hearing had deteriorated to the point where he could not catch words spoken quick and soft, "and it is not as if we could have kept it from him." She returned to comforting him and offering him assurances.

Jane then thanked Mr. Knightley for his assistance the night before.

"Think nothing of it," he said. "What are friends and neighbors for? I only wish the news had been better."

Mr. Perry, realizing that both Mrs. Churchill and Mr. Woodhouse might require his attentions, was the first of their friends to arrive at Hartfield. He had the excuse of his profession and so could come while they were still at breakfast. Mrs. Churchill declared that she needed nothing, and so Mr. Perry turned his ministrations to Mr. Woodhouse.

"You advise me to walk every day, but how can I do that, when murderers may be lurking in the shrubbery?" asked the frightened old man.

"My dear sir, if you like, I will walk with you," offered Mr. Knightley.

"You need to attend to your farm," said Mr. Woodhouse. "You cannot stay here protecting us all the time."

"Mr. Woodhouse, sir, how about if *I* walk with you today?" offered Mr. Perry.

"We will both walk with you, sir," said Mr. Knightley.

Mr. Woodhouse appeared reassured for the moment, then asked, querulously, "But what about tomorrow?"

"We will worry about tomorrow, tomorrow, Papa," said Emma, although she, like her father, was concerned about Mr. Knightley's being prevented from going to work on his farm. Yesterday there had been Mrs. Elton's musical afternoon; now there was the murder of Miss Bates.

Mr. Woodhouse was escorted by both his tall son-in-law, Mr. Knightley and his old friend Mr. Perry, for his after-breakfast walk, while Emma and Jane moved from the breakfast table to the large parlor. But before Emma could extract any additional information from Jane – not that she believed Mrs. Churchill would reveal anything to her – the front door opened and the Eltons arrived.

Emma was not pleased to see the Eltons, but as Mr. Elton had been with Mr. Knightley the night before, and as Mrs. Elton could claim a much longer friendship of Jane's, their appearance was understandable and she welcomed them in the parlor. Mrs. Elton accepted Emma's offer of a cup of tea but ignored everything else said by Mrs. Knightley and turned her attention to Jane Churchill.

"Jane – I mean, Mrs. Churchill – how are you, Jane? We are so very sorry such a thing has happened! Shocking, shocking! Never had anything similar in Maple Grove – well, there was the wife of the blacksmith who was killed by her husband when he was drunk, but they were lower class people, and one can ignore such things. But when the violence spreads to attacks on women of gentility! The daughter of a vicar! So near the church! Shocking, shocking! I am quite terrified to leave the house, Jane, without the protection of Mr. E."

"How was your musical afternoon? I was so sorry to miss it."

"Ah, yes, you were not feeling well," and Mrs. Elton, whose chagrin at Mrs. Churchill's absence had evaporated with news of the death of Miss

Bates. "Perhaps, given what happened, Mrs. Churchill, it was for the best…"

And then Mrs. Elton began a monologue worthy of the late Miss Bates, in which she praised the success of her musical afternoon, punctuating it with phrases expressing her concern for Mrs. Churchill's health and spirits and exclamations of horror about Miss Bates.

Mr. Elton agreed with his wife, sometimes saying, "Very true," and "Exactly so," but Emma thought the vicar looked fatigued and distracted. Well, he had had little sleep and it had to be unsettling to have a murder so close to his church.

Mr. Woodhouse, Mr. Knightley and Mr. Perry came back inside, with Mr. Perry escorting Mr. Woodhouse to a separate room – Mr. Woodhouse wished for an examination and Mr. Perry was, as always, ready to humor his old friend. A few minutes after that, the Westons arrived, for a change without their daughter – to Emma they were a most welcome support, especially as the appearance of the others seemed to at least slow the flow of Mrs. Elton's words. Mrs. Weston consoled Jane, offering gentle and unalloyed sympathy, while Mr. Weston was more practical. He told Jane that she ought to come stay with them at Randalls – but to Emma's surprise, Jane demurred, saying that now more than ever she needed to go through the things of her aunt and her grandmother. Mr. Weston frowned, as if he thought she was being unreasonable, but Mrs. Weston put her hand on her husband's arm in order to prevent him continuing that subject.

"Jane, have you contacted Frank yet?" asked Mrs. Weston.

"No, Mrs. Weston, not yet," Jane said. "There has not yet been time."

Mrs. Weston addressed her husband. "My dear, why don't you write to him? He should hear about this as soon as possible."

"I can write to him," Jane said.

"Of course you can, but you are not feeling well, and you are distressed by your aunt's death," said Mrs. Weston.

"I'll take care of it," said Mr. Weston.

"Very well," Jane said, and then with an additional effort, "Thank you."

Emma thought that Mrs. Churchill did not seem eager to contact her husband, but then reflected that there were many possible explanations for Jane's dispiritedness: the death of her aunt, her general fatigue, the late hour they had all gone to bed the night before, not to mention any after-effects from Mr. Perry's sleeping-draught. She reminded herself that she did not know Jane well enough to interpret all that young woman's looks and expressions.

Emma supplied Mr. Weston with paper, a pen and ink, and he sat down at a desk to write the note to his son.

"Jane, would it trouble you too much to talk about what happened?" asked Mrs. Weston.

"No – I am thinking about it all the time, anyway."

"Do we have any idea who did it?" Mrs. Weston asked. "Mr. Knightley, you discovered the body. Do you know anything more?"

"I was there too," said Mr. Elton, quickly claiming his share of the credit.

"Of course you were, Mr. E," said Mrs. Elton. "Last night, when he finally came home, he was in a state, let me tell you!"

"The whole thing seems impossible. I can't imagine that she was killed by anyone who knew her," volunteered Mr. Weston, writing rapidly at the writing desk.

"No, indeed!" exclaimed Mrs. Elton. "Dear Jane, everyone loved your aunt – the idea of someone wanting to kill her is impossible."

"But someone did kill her," Mr. Knightley pointed out. "Let us not speculate just now but try to determine what we know. Elton, Mrs. Elton, about what time did Miss Bates leave the Vicarage?"

"She stayed later than most of the others," said Mrs. Elton. "We offered her a ride in our carriage but she refused."

"More's the pity!" said Mr. Elton. "I should have insisted on walking her home – Mrs. Churchill, my deepest apologies, but when she left it was not quite dark."

"It is not your fault," said Jane, "how could you have any idea?"

"With the preparations for the musical afternoon, the household has been in an uproar and I wanted to choose my sermon for Sunday," Mr. Elton continued making his excuses.

Mr. Knightley persisted in ascertaining facts. "Shortly before dark," he said. "That was about five-thirty yesterday. Who else was still with you?"

Mr. Elton and Mrs. Elton exchanged a glance. "Miss Nash, Mrs. Goddard and her students were given a ride by the Coles. The Perrys and the Coxes had departed."

"What about the servants? And the young musicians?"

"The young musicians!" Mrs. Elton exclaimed. "Surely you don't suspect any of them – they are too young – oh, my! Dear Jane, I cannot imagine that it is so. No, Mr. Knightley! What you are implying is impossible!"

"Calm yourself, Augusta," said Mr. Elton, putting a hand on his wife's shoulder.

"I have no suspicions, yet, Mrs. Elton," said Mr. Knightley. "But I want to know who was where, when. I'm sure your young musicians are not killing women in churchyards – but one of them could have *seen* something, or someone."

"Ah – of course, of course," said Mrs. Elton, relaxing a little. "I am so upset just now, I can't remember. Let me think. You and Mrs. Knightley were the first to leave – and right after that the Westons – I *do* understand your deserting so early; I'm a mother as well. Others stayed to enjoy the cake, but perhaps half an hour later, everyone from Mrs. Goddard's school left with the Coles. The Perrys and the Coxes departed before Miss Bates, too. We wanted to talk to Miss Bates about the addition to the church in honor of her mother – she was very interested, Mrs. Churchill. Then she left. The servants – even the two we hired from the Crown – were still with us. They stayed another hour at least, washing and moving the furniture back into place."

"Miss Bates left shortly before five o'clock," said Mr. Knightley. "I think we can assume that Miss Bates was not visiting her mother's grave for very long, so that the servants who left another hour later could not have anything to do with the –" he hesitated, and glanced at Jane Churchill, as if concerned about her sensibilities, but after a second plowed on, "—with the attack on Miss Bates – or have even seen anything."

"What about the musicians?" asked Mr. Weston, who had finished his letter and was inserting the paper into an envelope.

Mrs. Elton frowned, as if trying to recall, and then said, "All the young musicians were gone, except for the two Draper girls, who were waiting to be met by their father and walked home."

"The gypsies," said Emma, in a low voice, but everyone turned and looked at her.

"Yes, the gypsies from Gilbert's farm," repeated Mr. Knightley. "When did their father arrive?"

"Draper arrived a few minutes after Miss Bates departed. I was glad to see him, for Mr. Elton was at the point of preparing to take out our carriage to take them home himself – they are too young to go so far alone. Not that they can't walk so far – they are sturdy types – but we just had the cushions cleaned," Mrs. Elton said.

"What sort of man is their father?" asked Mr. Weston. "This Draper?"

"You think *he*--?" asked Mr. Elton.

"Well, someone killed her," said Mr. Weston grimly.

"Oh, my word!" Mrs. Elton was half-hysterical at the suggestion. "To think we might have had a killer in the house! He entered our kitchen and we even gave him a few leftover biscuits to take home with him after the afternoon. I may have been speaking with a murderer!"

"Please calm yourself, Mrs. Elton," said Mr. Knightley. "We don't know that the girls' father is the culprit. Did you notice anything unusual about him when you spoke to him?"

"You mean, he could have killed Miss Bates before he came to my house?" Mrs. Elton asked, her voice rising.

"Do you think he took his daughters with him and killed her in front of them?" asked Mrs. Weston, aghast.

"What? No, I see what you mean, perhaps not – that would be too much, even for a man like him," said Mrs. Elton.

"What was Draper like when you saw him?" asked Emma, who had been listening to the conversation very carefully, but was also keeping an ear open for the return of her father.

Mrs. Elton, sitting straighter with all this attention, considered. "He was breathing hard when he came to the kitchen and his hands were a little dirty – he needed a shave – but I did not see any blood."

"Did you notice anything, Elton?" asked Mr. Knightley.

The vicar shook his head. "I congratulated Draper on how well his daughters performed. He thanked us for the opportunity and then took Florica and Kizzy away. I then went to my study and worked for several hours while Mrs. Elton supervised the servants as they cleaned up from the party."

"What about you, Weston?" asked Mr. Knightley. "Did you notice anything?"

"As Mrs. Elton already said, we left shortly after you did. Anne wanted to get back to our little girl, and I had some items of business from my brothers to review. I went to my study and worked late too."

"We noticed nothing," said Mrs. Weston.

They heard footsteps in the hall; Mr. Perry and Mr. Woodhouse were finished with their private business. They all fell silent, for everyone knew Mr. Woodhouse could not endure this sort of conversation. Emma was divided; in a way she wanted them all to depart, for she needed to take care of her father and her child and tend to her household, but on the other hand, she was extremely curious about what more might be said.

"We will have to investigate," said Mr. Knightley. "Weston, Elton – and Cole – we should meet at the Crown today and discuss what is to be done about this. Emma, could you write a note for me and send it around to Cole?"

"For what time?" Emma asked.

Mr. Knightley glanced at the clock. "Let us say three this afternoon. I must first go to Donwell. Weston, Elton, does that hour suit you?"

The other men acquiesced. "I will go to the post office with this note to Frank," said Mr. Weston. "Jane, can I escort you anywhere? If not to Randalls, then back to your grandmother's apartment?"

"I wish to consult with Mr. Perry," said Jane.

"What about the funeral?" asked Mr. Elton.

Jane sighed. "Of course, we must plan that."

Emma was struck by how a murder caused not only grief and fear, but so many other activities and inconveniences. "Would you mind going into another room for these discussions?" asked Emma. "I don't think my father's nerves are ready to listen to the details for a funeral."

Everyone was aware of Mr. Woodhouse's sensibilities. Mr. Weston left Hartfield to take the letter to the post office, while the Eltons and Jane Churchill went to the dining room, which had been cleared of its breakfast things, and sat at the large round table. Mr. Elton took out a pencil and a piece of paper and started making suggestions regarding the funeral service. Mr. Knightley assisted Mr. Woodhouse to his chair before the fire, while Mr. Perry took another seat.

"How are you, Papa?" Emma asked, knowing that *her* attentions were what her father required. "How was your walk?"

"I survived," said Mr. Woodhouse. "There was one point where I thought I heard someone in the shrubbery. I was absolutely terrified, especially when something dark came out."

A thrill of fear rushed through Emma. As Mr. Weston had said, *someone* had killed Miss Bates, and obviously they did not know who it was, so it was not impossible that a murderer lurked on Hartfield's property.

"It was only a pair of crows," Mr. Knightley assured everyone.

"Still, I was terrified."

"There is nothing to be afraid of, Papa," Emma reassured him, "it sounds as if you frightened the crows even more than they frightened you."

This pleasantry was unintelligible to Mr. Woodhouse; Emma decided it was too soon for wit.

"Would you like a cup of tea, Mr. Woodhouse?" offered Mrs. Weston.

"Yes, thank you, Mrs. Weston," said Mr. Woodhouse. "What a morning! What has happened to Highbury?"

No one could answer him. Mrs. Weston poured tea for Mr. Woodhouse, then served a cup to Mr. Perry; Mr. Knightley declined. "I will check on the others," Emma said, who was curious about the Eltons and Jane Churchill.

The others were concluding their business, Mr. Elton writing notes about which readings to include in the service – Miss Bates's favorite passages in the Bible – and Jane was nodding agreement. A grave would be dug beside her parents' although it was dreadful to think Miss Bates would be buried where she was killed.

"Is there anything I can get you?" asked Emma.

"Nothing, Mrs. Knightley," said Mr. Elton, putting the paper and the pencil in his pocket. "Mrs. Churchill, I will take care of these details for you."

"My dear Jane, come and stay with us," said Mrs. Elton. "At least until Mr. Frank Churchill comes to claim you."

"You are very kind, Mrs. Elton, but I must refuse," Jane said.

Mrs. Elton was mortified. "You mean to stay here with the Knightleys?"

"You are welcome to do so," Emma said.

"You are very kind, Mrs. Knightley, but—"

"Or the Westons? You ought to stay with them," said Mrs. Elton. Her perpetual competition with Emma meant that she could not endure Mrs. Churchill choosing to stay with the Knightleys in preference to herself, but the Westons were somewhat neutral territory, and of course Mr. Weston was Jane's father-in-law. If Jane chose to stay with the Westons that would be understandable and not showing any favoritism towards the Knightleys.

"You are very kind but I will return to the apartment, at least for the present."

Both the Eltons and Emma looked at Mrs. Jane Churchill as if she were mad. "Jane! I know our humble vicarage does not have the luxury that you are accustomed to in London or in Edgecombe, but our place has to be more comfortable than your late grandmother's cramped apartment."

"Or if you don't want to stay with us or the Knightleys – infants can make life inconvenient," said Mr. Elton, "then why not the Westons?"

"Thank you, but I am determined," said Jane. "I do not think I will be alone long. My – husband will be here later today, I am sure – tomorrow at the very latest."

"Are you not frightened?" Emma blurted out, for Jane's face was pale and looked frightened to her.

"A little, but I will take precautions to protect myself. Ah, Mr. Perry, there you are. Could I trouble you to escort me back to my aunt's apartment?"

Mr. Perry acquiesced, and then Jane thanked Emma and the Eltons and departed. The Eltons and Mrs. Weston left too – the mothers wanting to return to their young children, and Mr. Elton full of ideas for his Sunday sermon, which would have to be revised to reflect the evil that had come to Highbury. One of the Hartfield servants was dispatched to accompany Mrs. Weston the half-mile to Randalls. In the meantime, Emma had many questions for Mr. Knightley but was reluctant to raise them before her father. They went to the hallway to speak, as he put on his coat and prepared to depart.

"I need to get to Donwell Abbey, if only for a few hours," Mr. Knightley said. "The harvest cannot wait. After that I will meet with Cole, Elton and Weston to determine what we can do about this dreadful business. Will you be all right?"

"My father is very anxious," said Emma. "Someone has killed one of his oldest friends."

"I will not take the carriage. If James remains here, Mr. Woodhouse will not be as worried."

"For himself, perhaps, but what about *you?*" asked Emma.

"Do you really think *I* am in danger?" Seeing his wife frown, and remembering that there was a killer in the area, Mr. Knightley continued, "What if I ride instead of going by foot?"

"That would be better," Emma said. "And faster."

"Very well. We both have things to do – and I have that meeting at the Crown – but I will be home as early as I can."

"Will you tell me anything you find out?" Emma asked, wrapping his scarf around his neck.

"Yes," said Mr. Knightley.

"Do you have any suspicions?"

"Nothing that makes sense," said Mr. Knightley, pulling on his riding gloves.

"Do you mind if I develop some?" asked Emma.

"Not at all," said Mr. Knightley. "I would appreciate your imagination. This is a far more important subject than wondering why Mr. Elton has placed one of his own wine glasses on his own furniture. We will talk later, dear Emma."

16 WAITING, WORRYING AND WONDERING

Even after their visitors had left, the rest of the day at Hartfield was unsettled. Emma soothed her father, answered questions from the curious servants, and wrote responses to the many notes that were delivered by the servants of their Highbury neighbors. The frequent knocking at the front door made Mr. Woodhouse especially nervous, for he was afraid that the murderer, whoever he was, would come to Hartfield.

"I don't think that a murderer would knock," said Emma, easing her son's fist out of his mouth – Baby George persisted on sucking on his knuckles, which were now chafed and red.

"Why wouldn't a murderer knock?" asked Mr. Woodhouse. "It has to be the easiest way to get inside."

"Why would anyone want to kill us?" asked Emma.

"Why would anyone want to kill Miss Bates?" asked Mr. Woodhouse. "We're far more likely victims than Miss Bates!"

"Nonsense, Papa, everyone likes and respects you," said Emma. "And we are not out in a graveyard at night, but inside a large house with thick walls and a stout door." She refrained from mentioning that Miss Bates had probably been killed before dark.

But Mr. Woodhouse had his own retort to his daughter's argument. "The stout door is why the murderer will knock!"

Despite Mr. Woodhouse's concerns, Mrs. Knightley insisted on their doors being opened whenever someone knocked on them, the front as well as the service. And so, Emma learned later, the servants at Hartfield prepared to defend themselves with the tools of their respective trades: James the coachman with his horsewhip, the butler with the poker, and Serle the cook with a rarely-used waffle iron, as Mr. Woodhouse had refused to eat waffles for decades. After all, a murderer had been in Highbury the night before, and had attacked one of their village's most harmless citizens, so who could tell where danger lurked? It was best to be prepared. Even Emma imagined herself grabbing her baby and running through the house and out a side door – presuming the murderer came in through the front – or defending her father and her son with a large book or a heavy brass candelabrum.

So, the inmates of Hartfield were relieved when the person at the door turned out to be the familiar Mr. Perry arriving with an ointment for Baby George's red hand, or their beloved Mr. Weston with a report, early in the afternoon, that his son Frank was on his way to Highbury and that Miss Bates's funeral would be on Monday, or the usual deliveries of butter, coal and the post. And they were happiest, of course, when Mr. Knightley returned from his day at Donwell Abbey and his meeting at the Crown Inn, for not only was he safe, but everyone else at Hartfield felt safer.

They exchanged the news, mostly repeating what they already knew. Miss Bates's body had been taken to the undertaker and her funeral would be on Monday. Mr. Frank Churchill was on his way down from London to be with his wife; it was possible, given how fast he was on a horse, that he had already reached Highbury.

"Do you have any idea who killed her?" Mr. Woodhouse asked Mr. Knightley.

"No, sir," said Mr. Knightley. "Not yet."

"It still seems so impossible," said Mr. Woodhouse.

"Indeed, sir," agreed Mr. Knightley.

"Murder! In Highbury!" exclaimed the old man, and then turned to eating his dinner.

Emma, who wanted more than platitudes, but who did not want to upset her father further kept her questions to herself until later. "So, tell me: what are you doing to find out who did it?" asked Emma, when she and Mr. Knightley were finally alone.

Neither Highbury nor Donwell had a police force, as justice was usually meted out by local magistrates such as Mr. Cole, for Highbury, and Mr. Knightley, for Donwell. Kingston was the nearest town with a real constabulary. Once a criminal was determined to be a criminal, or at the very least a suspect, that person could be arrested and put into gaol, but determining who that person was, without witnesses or incriminating evidence, was an entirely different matter.

"As you know, I met with Cole, Weston and Elton," said Mr. Knightley. "We determined what we already know, which is not much, and decided what we will do to learn more."

"And what is being done?" asked Emma.

"Weston and Elton, as those who live nearest the churchyard, went over where the murder took place to see if they could discover anything more in the light of day. They learned little, though: the weapon seems to have been a piece of an old gravestone – in the sunlight they could see blood on it."

"So that is something," said Emma. "If the murderer used what was at hand, perhaps he did not come there planning to kill Miss Bates. Perhaps it was something that occurred to him at the moment."

"You may be right," said Mr. Knightley. "After all, who knew she would be there?"

"And who would want to kill Miss Bates? She was universally liked," said Emma.

"Not quite universally," Mr. Knightley corrected her.

"True, I found her tiresome, but I seem to be in a minority, and it is not as if I had to deal with her constantly. My motive is insufficient. Furthermore, when could I have killed her? You and I left the Vicarage together, before Miss Bates departed – and after that I did not stir from Hartfield, which you and my father and the servants all know."

"Do not fear; I do not suspect you."

"In fact I have not left Hartfield since the musical afternoon at the Eltons – which was only yesterday, but seems so long ago!" Emma remarked.

"Yes, it does," Mr. Knightley agreed, drinking some spruce beer. "Then tomorrow we will interview more people to see if anyone saw anything. Cole and Elton will talk to those near here – the servants hired from the Crown and the students from the school – while Weston and I will interview the shepherd boy who works for Robert Martin and the Draper girls at Gilbert's farm."

"And do you have any suspicions?" asked Emma.

"The gold locket that she was wearing is still missing. That was the real reason that Elton and Weston went to the cemetery: to see if they could find it. I thought there was always the possibility that it fell off of her last night. But they did not."

"So you think that she was murdered for the gold locket? Robbery, and then murder to cover it? Was it so valuable?"

"You mean, worth a woman's life? I don't think so, of course, but a thief might think differently."

"So in that case the murder of Miss Bates would have been the spur of the moment, instead of – what is the word? – premeditated."

"Yes, it seems that way. After all, the killer's weapon was already in the graveyard. But unless we find a witness – or find the locket on someone, we will not know who did it."

"Murder for the sake of robbery," said Emma, "how dreadful."

"It is. But it is better than Miss Bates's being killed by someone she knew."

"By someone she knew, which would mean someone we all know," said Emma. "Yes, that is even more horrible. Still, murder for robbery seems rather unlikely. How could a thief know she was wearing the locket? She had a coat, did she not? Her locket would not be visible if she was wearing a coat."

"You see why I am not entirely satisfied."

"Perhaps she lost it elsewhere," said Emma. "Perhaps she dropped it somewhere between the Vicarage and the churchyard."

"Perhaps," said Mr. Knightley. "But I asked Elton to keep his eyes open between his house and the churchyard; he said he found nothing."

Emma rubbed her nose, wondering. "Someone else may have found it," she said. "Perhaps someone – a child or a servant – found it early this morning and has decided to keep it."

"You see how many possibilities there are. You are right in that the murder because of robbery is not a completely satisfactory solution, which is why I want you to call on Mrs. Churchill."

"Why?"

"I want you to ask her if she knows of anyone who might have wanted to kill her aunt."

"Me! Mrs. Churchill might confide in another – perhaps in Mrs. Weston – but she will never choose to confide in *me*."

"Perhaps not. But last night she came *here*, Emma – she came to Hartfield instead of continuing to Randalls."

Emma had wondered about the same thing, but she said: "Highbury is closer to Hartfield than is Randalls."

"And that could be the only reason she came here. Still, if you talk to her, you might learn something," said Mr. Knightley, yawning. "After all, you have a vivid imagination."

Emma still thought that it was a futile exercise, but she was not interested in having an argument. "Very well," she said.

The hour was late and of course Mr. Knightley's sleep had been disturbed the night before. So only a few minutes after they climbed into their bed, slumber claimed him. Emma, however, remained awake, thinking about Mrs. Churchill.

Mr. Knightley had reminded Emma how little she had cared to spend time with Miss Bates, an attitude which seemed to be shared by few others. But what if Emma's opinion of Miss Bates *was* shared by others, but the others simply hid it better? Jane Fairfax Churchill, even if she and Emma had never been intimate friends, had always struck Emma as extremely rational – more rational even than Emma. What if the prospect of having Miss Bates living with her for the next twenty years was more than Mrs. Churchill could bear? What if Mr. Frank Churchill had objected? He could have felt extremely oppressed – having survived one aunt who had made his life miserable for more than twenty years, only to now be facing the prospect of his wife's aunt, just as tiresome, moving in with them.

Indeed, Emma was wondering, if Mrs. Churchill could be the murderer. She could have arranged to meet her aunt in the churchyard – or perhaps she had *not* told her aunt this, as Miss Bates could certainly not have been trusted to hold her tongue – but had hidden herself in the churchyard, waiting for her aunt to appear after the concert. It could explain why Mrs. Churchill had decided not to go to Mrs. Elton's musical afternoon.

It was difficult, though, to imagine Mrs. Churchill lifting a heavy stone and hitting her aunt's head with it. True, Mrs. Churchill was taller and stronger than her middle-aged aunt, yet nevertheless the idea was challenging even for Emma's practiced imagination. It was easier to imagine Jane's husband as performing the deed – much as Emma liked Mr. Frank Churchill, finding him far more amusing than Jane – liking someone should not result in acquittal if that person were guilty of something so heinous. Of course, Mr. Frank Churchill, according to all accounts, had not even been in Highbury. But what if that was a lie? What if there was another reason that Mrs. Churchill had stayed away from Mrs. Elton's musical afternoon? Perhaps she had expected her husband to join her, and they were planning to kill Miss Bates?

Emma's theories explained some of the facts – but not all. If Jane Churchill truly disliked living with her aunt, then why had she chosen to stay with her these past few weeks? She could have easily said her visit was complete and returned to her husband. Nor did she have evidence that Miss Bates had been planning to leave Highbury and move in with the Churchills. If that had been contemplated, Miss Bates, the soul of indiscretion, would surely have mentioned it. Emma had to admit to herself that Mr. and Mrs. Churchill's motives were not very strong.

Mr. Knightley snored, turned over, and Emma yawned. The murder of Miss Bates, though horrible, was the most interesting thing ever to happen in Highbury – not that she would admit *that* inappropriate attitude to anyone – but she needed sleep before she continued puzzling through it.

17 CONDOLENCE CALLS ON THE CHURCHILLS

The next day Emma went to Highbury to call on Mrs. Churchill. As she had told her husband, she doubted very much that Jane Churchill would tell her any secrets, but she was curious. Mr. Woodhouse approved, too, as long as James the coachman escorted her to Highbury.

"You will tell her how very distressed we are at what happened to her aunt," said Mr. Woodhouse. "Shocked and distressed. Never has such a thing happened in Highbury! Never, indeed!"

"Yes, Papa."

"She should not be alone," Mr. Woodhouse continued. "She should go to Randalls, or even come here to stay. She is a quiet young lady, and would be no trouble at Hartfield."

"I expect she is not alone, Papa," Emma said. "I expect that her husband has come down from London to be with her."

"Ah, yes, Mr. Weston's son. Well, if Mr. Frank Churchill is with her, I am sure she will be safe. Still, she will like to see you, Emma. Your visit will comfort her."

"Yes, Papa," she said, wondering why everyone was so convinced that Mrs. Churchill would be happy to see her when there was so little evidence to support that supposition. Nevertheless she went, accompanied by James the coachman, to Highbury. They did not take out the carriage and horses as the distance was so short and because leaving the Woodhouse carriage before the building with the Bates apartment was inconvenient to passers-by. The building's ground floor was a bakery and hence people were always going in and out.

Emma and her coachman walked mostly in silence, but when they passed the Crown Inn, James, peering into the courtyard, commented on Mr. Churchill's carriage within. "That Mr. Churchill's got a nice pair of bays," he said, looking about, "I expect they're being rubbed down by one of the stable boys."

So, Mr. Frank Churchill *was* here, thought Emma. She wondered if she could get confirmation regarding when he had arrived. "If you like, you can take a look at them," she said to James. "I can find my way to the Bates apartment from here."

"No, Mrs. Knightley, I'll do my job and take you to the door," said James. "But while you're inside I will come back and take a look at the bays. They're handsome horses, they are."

Emma was loath to inquire more directly. James escorted her to the building in which the Bateses had lived and she went up the stairs, where she knocked and was admitted by Patty, the woman who had served Mrs. Bates and her daughter for decades.

Mr. and Mrs. Frank Churchill were at home, but not alone; Mrs. Perry and Mrs. Weston were visiting.

"Mrs. Knightley – how good of you to call," Mrs. Churchill said.

"All of us at Hartfield – my father, my husband and myself – have been concerned about you," Emma said.

"I am as well as I can be."

The conversation continued. Emma greeted Mr. Frank Churchill, whose natural cheerfulness was subdued – not surprising, given the seriousness of the events.

"I came down at once," he said, and explained that he had departed from London as soon as he received the news. "My uncle is not well, but I left immediately and arrived late yesterday."

"My coachman and I saw your carriage at the Crown," Emma said.

"Yes, I brought the carriage because I hope to persuade Jane to come back with me. After the funeral, of course."

"I need to remain in Highbury a little longer," said Jane, shaking her head. "There are matters to settle."

"Then why not come and stay with us at Randalls?" suggested Mrs. Weston.

"Please, I wish to stay here, in the apartment that was home to my aunt and to my grandmother. To me it is important."

"Are you not frightened?" asked Mrs. Perry.

Jane smiled – a strange smile, thought Emma. "What reason have I to fear? My aunt was killed – it is such a horrible thing – during a robbery near the church. Do you really think anyone will break into this building – so humble in its appearance – to attack me?"

Emma sensed that Mrs. Churchill would not be moved, and so offered her support. "I cannot imagine criminals coming up those stairs," she said. "If you need anything while you are here, let us know at Hartfield."

Jane thanked her, and asked Emma to convey her gratitude to Mr. Knightley as well, for their assistance the other night.

"We are at your disposal whenever you need us."

Just then Mrs. Elton, puffing, knocked on the door. Emma decided to keep her visit brief; besides, Jane had already voiced her theory about her aunt's murder, and Emma did not think she would learn anything more. So she departed, leaving the Churchills to be condoled by Mrs. Elton, whose specialty this was, and went back down the dark, narrow staircase. Just outside she found James waiting for her, and the two of them walked back to Hartfield. A few discreet inquiries on her part, and she determined that Mr. Churchill had arrived yesterday evening in his carriage, as he had said. James had even spoken with Mr. Frank Churchill's coachman, so there seemed to be no question.

That evening, Emma and Mr. Knightley shared what they had learned. She was the first to report. "Mrs. Churchill believes her aunt was murdered for the locket. If she has any other thoughts on the matter, she would not share them with me – or at least not in front of so many other people."

Mr. Knightley grunted. "And? What else is bothering you?"

"Mrs. Churchill wants to remain in the Bates apartment." She explained how Frank wanted her to return with him to London; how Mrs. Weston had pressed her to come to Randalls; how Mrs. Perry had wondered how Jane could bear to remain by herself. "She repulsed every invitation and denied every objection. She cannot want to stay in Highbury to keep her aunt company – Miss Bates is dead – but she is determined to remain where she is."

"What reason did she give?"

Emma repeated what Mrs. Churchill had said: how she wished to remain in Highbury to go through the things of her grandmother and her aunt, and how staying in the apartment allowed her to feel close to them.

"Mrs. Churchill is a woman of deep feeling," Mr. Knightley remarked.

"Perhaps," Emma said. "Did you interview the Drapers? And Martin's shepherd?"

Mr. Knightley, as promised, related what he observed when he went to see the Gilberts. Mr. Weston had gone with him, which worked well, as Mr. Weston as a young man had served in the army – he had been Captain Weston then – and Noah Draper, they had learned, had briefly been in the infantry. "A little extra authority always helps with these fellows," opined Weston. He could not wear his saber – that would look silly; and his red coat was now too small and anyway out of style – but he carried his old pistol in his belt.

They went on horseback to the Gilbert estate, speaking first to Mr. Gilbert, who assured Mr. Knightley that the families working for him on the harvest had worked for him for several years now – and that he had never had trouble with them before. He grew rather defensive.

"We are not accusing Draper," Mr. Knightley told Gilbert, "but they were in the area at about the right time. He or one of his daughters might have seen something. All we want to do is to question them."

Gilbert could not find a reason to deny Knightley's request, so he arranged for Noah Draper, and his daughters, Florica and Kizzy, to come to the kitchen to be interviewed.

"You did not go into their quarters?" asked Emma.

"No, Gilbert said they had been angry ever since my last intrusion. They value their privacy, He values them – even the girls work hard – and he was not going to risk offending them again."

"But they could be hiding evidence! Miss Bates's locket and even your silver!"

"That's what Weston said."

"And if you postpone looking for evidence, they could get rid of it!" Emma continued.

"Again, Weston agreed with you. Still, I thought it better to go along with Gilbert's wishes. He's a good man, Gilbert is, and as a fellow farmer I understand how dependent he is on good help during the harvest season."

More important than finding a murderer? Emma wondered, but held her tongue. She appreciated her husband's passion for farming, for in truth it was both noble and necessary, as without farmers they would all starve – yet sometimes he seemed to elevate farming beyond its just desserts. Still, she would not have *that* discussion now. "So the man and his two daughters came to you in the kitchen," she prompted.

"Yes," said Mr. Knightley, and related the conversation.

" 'I know why yer here,' said Mr. Draper. 'You think I had something to do wi' the woman who got herself killed in the church graveyard.'

"I explained that we had only come to see if he knew anything, if he had seen anything.

" 'Nay, you want to make me out to be the guilty party. Can't stand to think that one of yer rich friends in one of yer great houses might be guilty. Well, I ain' havin' none of it!'

" 'Dad, please,' said the elder Miss Draper. 'He hasn't accused you of anythin' yet.'

"Draper then vented his irritation on his daughters. 'If you an' Kizzy hadn't taken it upon yerselves to go singin' our songs in the house of that minister-man and his nose-in-the-air wife, we wouldn't be in this spot. She was too miserly to give you a few coins or even a ride home in her carriage, even though yer young and shouldna' have to walk that far – only a few stale tarts, an' only those because they had too many of them.' "

Emma could not help laughing at this portrayal. "Perhaps it is just as well that Mr. Weston, and not Mr. Elton, was with you."

"I only repeat Draper's words to demonstrate that you, Mrs. Knightley, may have more in common with Noah Draper than you realize. At least you share a similar opinion of Mrs. Elton."

"Indeed," Emma said archly, not liking to be compared with a poor, uneducated itinerant farm worker, but not wanting to interrupt her husband's description of what happened. "Pray continue."

" 'Mr. Draper,' Weston insisted, 'if you don't answer Mr. Knightley's questions, we will have to assume you were up to no good.'

" 'Like I said, these folk have already assumed I'm guilty!'

" 'Please, calm yourself,' said Mr. Gilbert.

" 'But he jest said…'

" 'All I want to know is where you were and what you saw. You and your daughters would have walked past the church graveyard. Did you see or hear anything?'

"Draper glared sullenly at me and then peered intently at Mr. Weston. 'Nothing,' he said at last.

" 'But, Dad—' started Kizzy, the younger Miss Draper.

" 'You shut yer mouth, girl!' barked her father. 'We saw nothin',' he announced blandly."

Mr. Knightley then explained that he thought that the girls might tell him more if he could question them alone, but not too surprisingly, Gilbert was against that. So was Mr. Weston, and another look at the girls' frightened faces made him decide against pressing for it.

The Drapers then left the kitchen, and the Gilberts, Mr. Knightley and Mr. Weston went to the parlor.

" 'Sorry about that,' said Farmer Gilbert. 'But I don't think they have much to say. And they won't talk to you, Mr. Knightley.'

" 'Perhaps they'll talk to you?' I asked. 'Or the girls might talk to Mrs. Gilbert?'

" 'That's more likely,' said Gilbert. 'I know they're rough and they keep to themselves but I've never had an iota of trouble with them. And why would they kill Miss Bates? It makes no sense.'

"We thanked them for their time, and apologized for any distress we might have caused. Then Weston and I left, agreeing that it had not been the most productive of visits. I stopped to check on things at Donwell Abbey while Mr. Weston rode on home to Randalls."

"I have to agree, the interviews were not that useful," said Emma, rather disappointed. She wished that she had been there herself, for she was certain that she would have noticed something that would have indicated either innocence or guilt. "And the shepherd youth who works for the Martins?"

"He left well before Miss Bates," said Mr. Knightley. "Robert Martin said the youth returned before dark."

"So he had no useful information."

"None at all," said Mr. Knightley.

Emma shook her head; she felt as if they were groping in the dark.

18 ANOTHER BATES FUNERAL

The next day was Sunday; the day after that Monday and the funeral of Miss Bates. The attendees were virtually the same as those who had come to the funeral for her mother a few weeks ago. That service was marked by solemn serenity; the one for the daughter, by horror and shock. Everyone still wondered how murder could have found its way to Highbury. At the reception at the Crown afterwards – so similar in the food and the persons present – people were tense.

The Gilberts came to the funeral and the reception and reported that the Drapers had vanished the day before.

"What?" Mr. Knightley asked.

"Yes, they are gone."

"That sounds guilty," said Mr. Elton.

"Indeed it does," said Mr. Weston grimly.

Emma, listening, had to agree.

Mr. Gilbert maintained that he did not believe that Noah Draper had anything to do with the death of Miss Bates.

Mr. Woodhouse, who had consented to come to the Crown Inn again, asked for an explanation. Mr. Weston explained that they had gone to question the gypsies staying on the Gilbert property in connection with the killing of Miss Bates, but that those gypsies had fled.

"But that is good," said Mr. Woodhouse.

"How is it good, sir?" Mr. Knightley demanded.

The old man turned with relief. "It means that the dangerous criminals are gone," he said with satisfaction. "Highbury is as safe as it should be."

"Well, sir, that is a possibility," agreed Mr. Knightley.

"Certainly a mysterious departure is not a sign of innocence," said Mr. Weston.

"No, but the two of you made him feel guilty. He may have departed rather than risk a miscarriage of justice," said Mr. Gilbert.

"Miscarriage of justice!" exclaimed Mr. Weston hotly. "Who here could think that Mr. Knightley would be anything but just?"

"No reflection on you, Knightley," said Mr. Gilbert. "These fellows, though, they experience prejudice all the time. Draper would not trust any magistrate in any county in England."

"I understand," said Mr. Knightley.

"Still, if we know who did it, that's a good thing," said Mr. Weston. "Jane will be relieved," and he left their group to go to speak to his son, daughter-in-law and wife, who were standing in another part of the room.

"If Draper has gone, how are you for labor?" asked Mr. Knightley. "Do you need help? Should I send over William Larkins?"

"I'll manage," said Mr. Gilbert, rather shortly, "but that reminds me, we must go now." And he turned on his heel and left them.

"Why don't we leave too?" suggested Mr. Woodhouse.

The Knightleys agreed that they had no reason to stay. Mr. Knightley went to summon the carriage – Mr. Woodhouse could not walk the short distance from the Crown Inn to Hartfield – while Emma and her father paused to express their grief once more to the Churchills.

"A fine woman, your aunt," said Mr. Woodhouse. "She will be missed."

"Thank you, sir," said Jane.

"She was one of the kindest women I ever met, Mrs. Churchill," Emma added.

"Thank you, Mrs. Knightley. Thank you for coming. Thank you for everything."

Although Jane had tears in her eyes Emma thought that Mrs. Churchill looked very relieved. As she helped her father towards the door and they climbed into the carriage, Emma considered what they had learned from Mr. Gilbert, and concluded, as her father had, that Draper's departure was a good thing. The best thing would have been for the murderer to be caught and hanged – but the next best thing was to have him disappear.

19 FINDING GOLD

After the funeral for Miss Bates – and the news about the fleeing of the Drapers – Emma was actually a little disappointed. The intriguing puzzle seemed to have been solved, but the solution was not particularly satisfactory, and she had fewer interesting thoughts to challenge her brains.

Her father, however, was quite relieved, and so emboldened by the disappearance of the man they assumed to be the murderer, that he was able to walk in his own shrubbery without accompaniment later that afternoon.

Mr. Knightley announced that he would spend the following day at Donwell Abbey, and Emma, a little bored and very restless, volunteered to go with him. "I can finally see the cider press you have mentioned so often."

Her husband was pleased by her interest but suggested that she not come with him in the morning, which was when he intended to go, but follow in the afternoon with the carriage. "You should visit Harriet."

The next day they resumed their usual routine. Mr. Knightley departed early for his estate, and Emma spent time with her father and her son. Mrs. Weston stopped by with Anna and told her that after Hartfield, she was going to see her daughter-in-law Jane; Frank had departed yesterday for London. She confided that she was afraid that Jane would feel very lonely in the apartment and asked Emma to call on her too.

It did seem as if everyone was doing their utmost to push Emma Knightley and Jane Churchill into intimacy, but on this day at least, Emma had an excuse to postpone it. She had promised Mr. Knightley that she would drive out to Donwell Abbey. Mrs. Weston did not press, and departed with her little girl, while Emma ordered the carriage.

The day was very fine; the sky bright blue, without a single cloud. She glanced at laborers in the orchards and the fields; most of the apples and root vegetables had been gathered. Life had returned to normal; she thought; everyone was relieved but her.

The carriage lurched to a halt shortly before the Abbey-Mill Farm; instead of continuing, James opened the door.

"Is something wrong?" she asked.

"Mrs. Knightley, the carriage needs fixing. I'd rather not drive it with you in it until it's done."

"Ah," she said. "Then help me out, James."

She descended and they decided that he would continue to Donwell Abbey, which had the tools for repairing the carriage. "I don't know how long it'll take, mum."

"I will walk from here to Donwell Abbey," she said.

"Mum, are you sure?"

"Yes," she said, "go and mend the carriage, James."

Emma then called again on Harriet, and again found her friend suffering – although this time she entered the house without causing her friend to break anything. With alacrity Emma set the place to rights, made a pot of tea, and even rinsed some dishes.

"I don't know how to thank you," said Harriet, almost in tears. "I am so tired, and so queasy, and the babies are always crying. And now we have learned that Robert's mother is seriously ill – dying – so she will not be returning to help. And Elizabeth has decided to accept the offer of marriage from William Cox – so she will be not coming back either, at least not to live with us."

"As long as you don't tell anyone how poorly I do these things," said Emma, wiping her hands. "You need help that is constant and competent – better than my occasional visits. If Mrs. Martin is dying and Miss Martin is getting married, you must find someone else. Is there any girl who could come and work for you? Seriously, dear Harriet, can your husband afford it?"

"I don't know. He'll think I'm a failure. Mrs. Martin did not have this sort of help."

"Mrs. Martin did not have twins," Emma said crisply. Then she added, more thoughtfully: "Perhaps some young girl, willing to train – at least until you're feeling better – and the twins are a little older. And then one day, when you are feeling better, Harriet, I will send the carriage for you and the babies and you can spend a day or two at Hartfield. My father would love to see you."

"It sounds wonderful," Harriet admitted.

Emma then asked if Harriet had seen any sign of anything dangerous at her back gate – or at her front.

"No. Perhaps it is only because I am too sick to feel frightened. But the death of Miss Bates was terrible."

They discussed the murder of Miss Bates, and gossiped for a little while about the Churchills, and then Emma excused herself, as she was walking to Donwell Abbey. "At some point we will be close neighbors, Harriet – when I move to Donwell Abbey. And I must go there now, my friend."

"Good-bye, Mrs. Knightley," said Harriet, and then little Lizzie began to cry, distracting her poor mother.

Emma let herself out the front door. She had never walked this way before, so at least the endeavor had the veneer of novelty. Generally novelty, avoided by her father as dangerous, was absent from her life – but not these days!

What a great distance it was - how long these fields were. How far was it – half a mile? No, it could not be so far. And Mr. Knightley walked further, much further, every day. The young Draper girls had walked from the Vicarage to the Gilbert farm – a much greater distance. Even gentlewomen took long walks. Emma remembered how, after one summer afternoon picking and eating strawberries at Donwell Abbey, Jane Churchill – Jane Fairfax back then – had insisted on walking by herself all the way back to Highbury. Well, if Jane Fairfax could walk such a great distance without complaining, then Emma Woodhouse Knightley could manage the much shorter distance from the Abbey-Mill Farm to Donwell Abbey.

Some people, Emma thought, actually liked exploring. Jane Fairfax Churchill had inherited her grandmother's interest in nature. Emma tried to be interested in the dandelions scattered before the hedgerows – but she preferred well-kept houses. Still, perhaps she would see something interesting – there was a pretty leaf – a fuzzy caterpillar – eventually she would be taking her son George around here. *He* would be interested in everything, from the smallest pebbles to the largest trees.

Suddenly this walk seemed more interesting, pretending to see it through her son's eyes. Perhaps Baby George had inherited her imagination., her curiosity. He would ask her the name of the flower – the tree – the caterpillar. And then he would want to know if fairies and leprechauns hid gold in the woods; she imagined explaining to him that leprechauns lived in Ireland, not Surrey. Then he would say that there, not too far from the road, lay something shiny. He would insist on picking it up, hoping to find a coin. Emma's sister Isabella might try to restrain her boys, talking about dirt and disease, but Emma was more relaxed about such things. In fact, now *she* was curious about what glittered at the base of the lightning-struck beech tree.

Emma picked up a branch and went to the beech tree and scratched at the dirt before the hollow with it. There was something shiny – something real, not a trick of fairies or leprechauns – more than a coin – a chain of gold.

Emma gasped, dropped the branch – then bent down and picked up Mrs. Bates's golden locket.

*

"What do you think?" asked Emma later, showing it to Mr. Knightley as they rode in the now-fixed carriage from Donwell Abbey. "It *is* Mrs. Bates's locket, isn't it?"

"I need to examine it in better light, but I believe it is hers," Mr. Knightley said. "Where exactly did you find it, Emma?"

"In a moment, I can show you," she said, watching out the window. "There," she said, "just in front of the tree that was struck by lightning."

Mr. Knightley tapped on the ceiling of the carriage; James pulled the horses to a halt.

"Is something wrong, Mr. Knightley?" asked the coachman, as Mr. Knightley stepped out and then turned to assist his wife. "Is the carriage giving you trouble?"

"No, James, the carriage is riding fine. But Mrs. Knightley wishes to show me something."

Emma led her husband back to where she had dug up the locket. "Right there," she said, pointing at the ground, "I found it right there."

Mr. Knightley surveyed the area, walking around the tree, looking inside the hollow and all around. "Very well spotted, Emma," he said. "Nothing inside the tree – no other dirt in the area appears disturbed."

"You were hoping to find your silver?"

"A vain hope. Come, it is getting dark," he said.

They returned to the carriage and James continued driving them home, discussing, as the horses pulled them towards Hartfield, who could have placed the locket there.

"Do you think it was put there by Miss Bates's killer?" Emma asked.

"Probably," said Mr. Knightley, taking his handkerchief out of his pocket and using it to clean the locket.

"But why? If the killer wanted to sell it, then why bury it?" Emma wondered. "Of course, by putting it at *that* beech tree, so easy to recognize, he could easily locate it again. So perhaps the killer was not in a position to sell it during the last few days. And perhaps he did not want to keep it with him because he was afraid that it would be discovered among his things – and that would incriminate him."

"There seems to be no need for you to ask *me* questions, Emma, as you are answering them yourself."

"Ah, but I do not know if these are the right answers, Mr. Knightley. I don't even know if they are the right questions."

"But they are a good start. In general I would like to know: if the locket was placed there by Miss Bates's killer, what does that tell us about him?"

"Or her," Emma mused.

"A woman? Nonsense – surely Miss Bates was not killed by a woman," said Mr. Knightley.

"Do you think women are incapable of murder?"

"Not at all. But I think women, if they kill, tend to use poison, such as arsenic. Miss Bates, however, was hit on the head with a large stone – an act which required considerable strength. What woman do you know who is strong enough – brutal enough – to lift a heavy rock and then use it to hit poor Miss Bates with such force as to kill her?"

"You have a point," Emma said.

"But back to the matter of the locket. If we assume it was buried at the beech tree by the killer, then that means the killer must have passed along that road. And might be planning to come past here again."

The carriage lurched over a bump in the road, and Emma's stomach seemed to jump at the same time. "That means that the killer could still be in the area," she said.

"Exactly. The killer stood where you stood, Emma. I do not want you walking along that road again – at least not until we know he has been apprehended."

Mr. Knightley spoke with such gravity that Emma shivered. She recollected how terrified Harriet had been of the strangers she had seen walking along the path behind the Abbey-Mill Farm. Harriet might be silly; she might be so fatigued that she could barely see straight – but Harriet was not a complete fool and she was sensible to intense feelings in others. What if Harriet had sensed something dangerous, someone evil, behind her house?

She made these ideas intelligible to Mr. Knightley; he nodded. "I am worried. But still, Emma, if we could keep your father from becoming too anxious…"

"I understand," Emma said. She glanced out the carriage window; they were nearing Hartfield. "What should we do with the locket?" she asked, as they went through the iron sweep-gate.

Her husband looked at her with surprise. "Return it to Mrs. Churchill, of course."

20 SKETCHES FROM THE PAST

The next day the weather was windy, with clouds gathering in the west. Emma put on thick boots and a warm cloak and then walked to Highbury, the Bates locket wrapped in tissue and in her reticule. The distance to Highbury was short, and soon she was surrounded by the village houses and buildings, all full of friendly people. Even if one of them was a killer, others would rush to help her if she called out for help.

Still, her fears made the most innocuous appear sinister. What other crimes were happening in Highbury? Were there undetected poisonings, as Mr. Knightley suggested? Were other articles of silver being stolen? Even Mr. Cole, chatting with Mrs. Stokes in front of the Crown Inn, looked dangerous.

She was as bad as Harriet, thought Emma, opening a door and climbing a staircase to the Bates's apartment. She supposed she should consider it the Churchill apartment now – and even it would not retain that title for long, as Mrs. Churchill would surely not continue renting it.

As was usual, Emma heard voices before she reached the apartment door. She paused to listen, and for once felt she was being rewarded instead of being punished, as she discerned the friendly voices of Mr. and Mrs. Weston.

She knocked, and was admitted by Patty. "Mrs. Knightley," Mrs. Churchill said, "come in and join us."

Emma entered, and was happy to see that her ears had not misinformed her. Mrs. Churchill and Mr. and Mrs. Weston were working their way through a stack of papers.

"Emma, my dear, I am so glad to see you!" said Mrs. Weston. "We are looking over sketches – better than sketches – made by Mrs. Bates."

Emma handed her hat and coat to the servant and took a seat. "I did not know that Mrs. Bates drew."

"I have faint memories of her sketching when I was a child," said Mrs. Churchill, "but by the time that I left to live with the Campbells her eyesight had deteriorated. And so she stopped sketching."

Mrs. Weston was studying a sheet of paper. "Jane, some of these drawings are so natural!"

"Drawings of what?" asked Emma.

"Plants – and parts of plants. Emma, take a look at the detail of this leaf," said Mrs. Weston, passing the piece of paper to Emma.

Emma had to admire the artistic work. As someone with a little talent in drawing, she could appreciate the exactness of each stroke, the proportion, the shading, and the detail. Mrs. Bates's sketch of an oak leaf made her a little ashamed of her own want of application. "I prefer portraits myself, and can't imagine framing this for the mantelpiece, but naturalists would appreciate them. They are very precise."

"That is what I was thinking," said Jane, a little color in her cheeks, slightly more animated than usual. "She made notes about the plants in her journal – some of the ink is fading and I have been trying to make it out – but perhaps the Royal Society would appreciate these notes and drawings."

"Your grandmother was another Pliny!" said Mrs. Weston. "Mr. Weston, perhaps you could talk to someone in London about making engraved plates. Doesn't your brother know someone who works in publishing?"

Mr. Weston frowned. "Would you really want to expose Mrs. Bates in that way? How do you think she would feel about it? She was always a modest woman, the wife of a vicar, who preferred to be anonymous."

"Nonsense!" said his wife. "First, I can't believe that Mrs. Bates would mind – women are not as retiring as you believe, Mr. Weston, and second, she is deceased – it cannot possibly bother her. Besides it is not as if these are going to cause a scandal of any sort, or even much notoriety – they are of leaves and flowers, not portraits – and if Jane prefers they can always be submitted anonymously. But they are excellent and should not be hidden from view. Emma, look at this violet. Isn't it well done?"

Emma praised the sketch of the violet.

"My grandmother was very talented, and if these drawings would help naturalists, then why not?"

"Perhaps it would do no harm," said Mr. Weston. "At least some of them. Very well, I can take the papers and send them to my brother in London."

"I must sort through them first," said Jane. "That is one of the reasons I am staying here now, to explore Surrey and add notes and explanations to her drawings."

Emma wondered if this were the real reason Jane was remaining in Highbury, for how hard could it be to pack up Mrs. Bates's papers and take them with her to London? Or at least to Randalls, if it was truly necessary to stay in Surrey?

To keep herself from posing impertinent questions, Emma changed the subject. "Mrs. Bates was so talented, that I almost forgot why I came here today," she said, opening her reticule and taking out the locket, wrapped in paper, and handing it across to Mrs. Churchill. "I found this by a tree between Donwell Abbey and the Abbey-Mill Farm. Isn't this your grandmother's stolen locket?"

"What?" exclaimed Jane.

Emma had expected the recovery of the locket to be greeted with happiness and joy: the return of a treasure gone missing. Yet Jane was pale, her eyes were wide, as if she had received some terrible shock. "I thought you would be glad to recover it," she said.

Mrs. Weston remonstrated gently: "Emma, you forget the circumstances which led to its disappearance."

"Of course," Emma murmured. The locket had disappeared because Miss Bates had been murdered. Still, she could not see how she could be more delicate in returning it.

"Jane, do you have anything stronger than tea here? Brandy or sherry?"

Miss Bates had had no sherry or brandy, but there was a of bottle of cowslip wine, a gift from Mrs. Cole, who had made many bottles during the summer and given them to friends. Mrs. Weston wrinkled her nose a little at this, but sent Mr. Weston to fetch a bottle at Jane's direction.

Mr. Weston opened the bottle, found several glasses, and poured them each one, handing the first to Jane.

"I am so sorry that the return of the locket has distressed you," said Emma, lifting the glass to her nose and sniffing tentatively.

"I am not distressed," Jane denied.

"Where exactly did you find it, Emma?" asked Mr. Weston.

Emma, prompted by Mr. and Mrs. Weston, gave the details of her discovery. Jane, however, did not even seem to listen, but stared at a spot over the piano. Emma noticed that Mrs. Churchill's color had drained from her face; she was as pale as a wax doll.

"What a stroke of luck, to recover your locket this way," said Mr. Weston.

"I'm surprised you found it," said Mrs. Weston. "You'd think that if a thief truly wanted to hide treasure, he would have buried it deeper than you describe."

Emma explained that she thought that an animal might have dug after the thief.

Mrs. Churchill finally made an effort. She put down her glass of cowslip wine, untouched, and turned to Emma. "Indeed, Mrs. Knightley, I cannot thank you enough for returning this family heirloom to me. Your eyes are very sharp."

The thanks were given, but in a tone so wooden, that Emma felt as if Jane were telling her she was unhappy that she had found the locket. Offended, she decided that she had had enough. "I was glad to be of assistance," she said, forcing herself to be polite. "Your grandmother was a talented artist, Mrs. Churchill; I'm glad you have the locket to remember her by. I must return to Hartfield; my father and my son need me at home."

Emma left as quickly as she could, deciding that there was simply no pleasing Jane Churchill. They might be exactly the same age, both clever and talented, the two most attractive young matrons that Highbury could claim – but intimacy was beyond them. Emma had always felt guilty, responsible for the lack of friendship between them – but perhaps it was not her fault. Perhaps Jane had always disliked her more than she disliked Jane.

That conclusion was not particularly comfortable or reassuring but it did relieve Emma of the responsibility. She stepped over the threshold into Hartfield, happy to be inside as the clouds above were full of rain.

"Ah! Emma, my dear, there you are," said her father. "I feel much better when you are at home – when I know you are safe."

With a start she realized that, while reaching the conclusion that she and Jane Churchill would never be friends, she had forgotten about the anxiety which had plagued her on her way into Highbury. She kissed her father, told the servants to bring her a pot of tea and Baby George if he was awake. She was glad to be where she was confident that everyone liked her – even loved her. To make her situation even better, shortly after a few heavy drops splashed against the window panes, Mr. Knightley entered, returning from Donwell Abbey.

21 SEARCHING FOR THE LIGHT ON A DARK AND STORMY NIGHT

"You're home early," Emma said, glancing at the clock on the mantelpiece.

"No point trying to farm in this weather," he said. "When I saw what the clouds were doing, I started at once for Hartfield."

"Are your shoes dry?" inquired Mr. Woodhouse.

"They are now, sir, for I have changed them."

Their conversation was compelled to halt by a loud crash of thunder. "My, my," said Mr. Woodhouse, nervously. "A fierce storm, indeed."

"Usually the stronger the storm, the sooner it is over, Papa," Emma comforted him.

"I believe it will rain the rest of the day and well into the night," said Mr. Knightley, "but the lightning and thunder will be over soon."

They chatted for a while about the weather, discussing how long the storm would last. Mr. Knightley was correct in predicting that the thunder would dissipate quickly while the rain remained.

Emma inquired about the status of the harvest at Donwell. Mr. Knightley was satisfied and reported that nearly everything was in. "We have done better this year than most; there is always a struggle against the elements. But the crops that must be harvested are in. The root crops can wait."

The weather meant that night seemed to fall earlier than usual, and Mr. Woodhouse, rather like a bird whose habits were regulated by the sun, retired early. Even the baby fell asleep on his father's lap and was handed gently to the nursery maid to be taken to his crib. After that, Mr. and Mrs. Knightley remained in the parlor, enjoying the fire and the opportunity for intelligent conversation with each other.

"Did you go into Highbury? Was Mrs. Churchill glad to receive her grandmother's locket?" asked Mr. Knightley, who knew his wife would have something to say on these matters.

Emma described Jane Churchill's reaction to the return of the family heirloom. "She was not pleased, not at all," said Emma, still annoyed. "She stared at it as if it were a poisonous snake."

"Interesting," said Mr. Knightley, pouring himself a glass of port. "She sounds almost afraid."

Emma nodded slowly. "You are right, Mr. Knightley, she *was* afraid. But I don't know why. The return of her grandmother's locket must mean something to her – something we do not understand."

"Why don't you ask her?"

"Mr. Knightley, Jane Churchill is determined not to confide in me. I agree, she knows something – or at least suspects something. But I do not know how to break through her reserve. I have tried for years, and I have always believed the fault was mine. But I now think *she* does not wish to talk to *me*. If you have a suggestion on how I can overcome this, let me know."

He laughed. "Negotiating a peace treaty between two young women is beyond me; I have enough trouble dealing with criminals. You have done your best, Emma. Now, my dear, I am still not convinced we know what happened to Miss Bates, and I want to consult you on the matter. I will be methodical – you will apply your imagination – we will think and talk through what we know and suspect, and see if we make any progress."

Emma was delighted and intrigued. "How shall we proceed?"

"We will make a list of suspects, and consider the case against each one." He took out a pencil from his pocket, fetched a sheet of paper from the desk. "There's Noah Draper, but for various reasons I am not satisfied. Who else would you include?"

"Jane Churchill," Emma said promptly.

"Jane Churchill! You must be joking," said Mr. Knightley.

"No, I am not. And what about the Eltons?"

"The Eltons!" Mr. Knightley frowned. "Emma, this is supposed to be a list of possible killers, not people you do not like."

"I have my reasons, and I will give them to you," she said archly. "Do you wish to have the benefit of my imagination or not?"

"Very well," said her husband, and wrote, as she could see, 'The Eltons.' "I hope the servants are in bed and are not listening to this discussion."

"Do *you* have any suspects to add?"

"I do not."

"Well, if you come up with one – no matter how outrageous – I will listen."

"I do not see who could be more outrageous than Mrs. Churchill or Highbury's vicar."

"My father," Emma said promptly.

Mr. Knightley laughed again. "Your imagination is powerful, my dear."

"Only because I practice diligently."

"I assume we need not include Mr. Woodhouse? But let us be serious, dear Emma, and start by considering Noah Draper."

Case Against Noah Draper

Mr. Knightley reviewed his case against Noah Draper. The fellow was strong enough to kill Miss Bates, and because of the musical afternoon at the Eltons, they knew he had not been far from the churchyard when the murder took place.

"True," Emma agreed. "I have never met him, but is he a suspicious type?"

Mr. Knightley scratched his chin. "That is what I am afraid of, Emma. He accused me of being prejudiced, and perhaps I am. Perhaps I want him to be the guilty party because it is easiest and most comfortable."

"I admire your honesty with yourself," said Emma. "But he has disappeared, has he not?"

"Yes, and that seemed to speak to his guilt – or perhaps his lack of faith in my ability to perceive his innocence. Until you found the locket."

"Ah," said Emma, comprehending. "If he ran away, why not take the locket with him?"

"Just so, my dear. I could understand his burying the locket at the beech tree while staying with the Gilberts; there was always the chance that Mr. or Mrs. Gilbert would discover it, or one of his sharp-eyed daughters. But if he ran away, why not take it with him? It was not far from the Gilberts; he could have recovered it before departing, and it would have brought him a pretty penny."

"Those are very good questions, Mr. Knightley," Emma conceded. "But if he is not guilty, then why has he run away?"

"All I can conclude is that he, unfortunately, has no confidence in my impartiality. Can you think of another reason?"

"No. Everyone who knows you, Mr. Knightley, has faith in you, but this Draper does not know you."

Mr. Knightley explained that the other thing that always disturbed him about suspecting Draper was he did not see how Draper could know that Miss Bates was wearing a precious locket in the first place. To this objection, however, Emma had an argument.

"If he is a practiced thief, then he must have ways of determining who in the area had valuables worth stealing," she said. "There is enough gossip in Highbury – we all know each other's concerns – that he could have learned about Miss Bates and her mother's locket."

"Yes, but then why did he not take it with him when he left Gilbert's farm?" Mr. Knightley asked again.

"For that I have no answer," Emma replied. "And this makes me think that Jane Churchill agrees with you."

"What do you mean?"

"I think she was afraid when I returned the locket. She preferred, like we all did, to believe that Draper had killed her aunt. But now that the locket has been returned – and that the motive of robbery makes less sense – now she is afraid, because she has reason to suspect someone else."

Mr. Knightley conceded that his wife's arguments were sound. "Very well, let us consider your case against Jane Churchill."

Case Against Jane Churchill

Emma presented her arguments. Jane Churchill had not been at the musical afternoon at the Eltons, true, but that did not mean that she had stayed that afternoon in her apartment in Highbury. She would have known, too, that Miss Bates was planning to visit her parents' grave and could have waited for her in the churchyard.

Mr. Knightley said, "But Jane Churchill loved her aunt. Why would she want to kill her?"

Emma shared her ideas. They had always assumed that Jane Churchill had loved Miss Bates, but what if she had not? What if she had found Miss Bates as tiresome as Emma had found her? And what if Miss Bates had been pressuring her to let her come live with her and Frank in London?

"It may have been more than Jane could bear, and she could have decided that it would be easier to rid herself of her aunt."

"Hmm. And she stole the locket herself to make it look like robbery?" asked Mr. Knightley.

"Yes. Everyone knows about the theft of silver from your estate; it could have seemed opportune."

"But when could she have hidden it at the beech tree?"

"Anytime since the death of Miss Bates. Jane Churchill once told me she was not afraid to walk back alone from Donwell Abbey, so she could have just as easily walked there during the last few days. And if she knew she was the killer, she would not be afraid."

"It looks very black against Jane Churchill. Do you have anything to say in her defense?"

"I don't know how heavy the rock was that was used to kill Miss Bates. I don't know if she was strong enough to lift it. You picked it up, didn't you?"

"Yes, I did. A strong woman might have been able to lift it, but to wield it as a weapon? Dubious."

"Especially as Jane Churchill has never been known to be robust." Emma had a few more suspicions regarding Jane Churchill's health but out of female solidarity would not express them, not even to Mr. Knightley.

"So, it looks bleak for Jane Churchill, but you can find one ray of hope for her. What about her husband, Frank Churchill? He would be strong enough to lift that rock."

"True, but he was not in Highbury," Emma said.

"We only think he was not in Highbury."

"I had James check with the grooms at the Crown Inn – Mr. Frank Churchill arrived in his carriage only the day after Miss Bates was killed – and that was confirmed by Mr. Churchill's coachman."

"You have been thorough in your investigation, Emma," said Mr. Knightley. "Very well, what about your favorite enemies, the Eltons?"

Case Against the Eltons

Emma admitted that she had devised a case against the Eltons because she disliked them. Still, there were several points against them. Miss Bates had been in *their* house shortly before she was killed, and had been killed in the graveyard just beside the church. What if she had not left alone, as they had claimed, but if Mr. Elton had volunteered to escort her home? That would have been most gentlemanly on his part – perfectly natural. Then he could have killed her beside her parents' grave. "And Mr. Elton is strong enough to lift that rock."

"I agree that Mr. Elton could have killed Miss Bates, probably more easily than anyone else," said Mr. Knightley, sipping from his glass. "But what I can't understand is why he would do it."

Emma nodded. "True. Theft? Once at the Bates's apartment, he seemed very interested in the locket."

"Perhaps. But we were just at the Vicarage and saw no symptoms of financial trouble. And if he stole the locket because he wanted the gold, then why hide it so far away?"

"Because – because he was afraid the servants would see it. Or perhaps he hid it in a way that someone might find it and implicate Noah Draper."

"The latter seems rather far-fetched, Emma."

"At least we know that it would have been possible for him to hide it. As a vicar, Mr. Elton travels all around the area. And he obviously knew the situation of the Drapers, as Mrs. Elton had the girls sing for us."

"Again, you make it very clear *how* he could have done it, but I am still at a loss as to *why* he would do it. And if Elton hid the locket by the beech tree in order to implicate Noah Draper, then he did not steal it for material gain. In which case I can't see why he would kill her at all."

"You are right. The only reason I can come up with is that Miss Bates might have known some dark secret about the Eltons, and he killed her to silence her."

"Killing Miss Bates would be the only way to silence her – but 'unknown reason' is a weak argument, Emma."

"True. And if the Eltons might have had an unknown reason to kill her, then the same could apply to any other person in Highbury. Except –"

"—except what?"

"If Jane Churchill suspected the Eltons, it would be one more reason why she came to Hartfield that evening, instead of continuing to the Vicarage."

"Perhaps. Perhaps she only came here because Hartfield was closer. At the very least Jane Churchill is not sitting in her apartment in Highbury, inventing a case against us."

"I think not. And certainly she trusts you more than Noah Draper does!"

"If your second theory is correct, and she is the murderess, it actually means she thinks very little of my understanding," said Mr. Knightley, scratching his chin. "This is all very interesting, Emma, but although I feel the truth is swirling around us, I don't know what it is."

"Nor do I," Emma admitted.

"Your imagination is making me dizzy." He rose and tended the fire. "Let's go to bed, Emma. Perhaps the answer will come to us in our dreams."

22 MRS. BATES'S MUSHROOM

The next morning the storm was over. Mr. Knightley explained that he had a meeting at the Crown in the afternoon, and he left immediately after breakfast for Donwell Abbey. The sun was bright and strong; by mid-morning only a few determined puddles remained. Even Mr. Woodhouse found the path dry enough for exercise, and, at her usual time in the morning, Mrs. Weston dropped by with her little girl. They discussed the weather and the children, and finally, when Mr. Woodhouse had had enough attention, Mrs. Weston settled beside Emma while Anna chased dust motes in a sunbeam and Emma's little boy watched her with envious fascination.

"It seems we have no time to chat these days, dear Emma," said Mrs. Weston.

"We saw each other only yesterday," Emma pointed out, "but I know what you mean."

"Yes, over at Jane's."

"How is Mrs. Churchill?" Emma asked.

"I don't know, Emma. I really don't know."

"Something about her is bothering you, Mrs. Weston. If you wish to discuss it, you may be assured of my discretion."

"Perhaps you have not noticed – nay, I am sure you have – that Jane has been behaving oddly. Up until this week her separation from Frank was understandable, but now Mr. Weston and I are both very concerned. She has not set a day for returning to be with Frank, and she declines to move to Randalls. We do not understand her determination to be independent."

Emma could finally ask the question she had wished to ask ever since the conversation she had overheard after the funeral of Mrs. Bates. "Could there be a problem in their marriage? Are they unhappy?"

"She claims not, and he claims not, but I suspect they are not telling Mr. Weston and me the truth."

"They hardly have a reputation for complete honesty," Emma remarked.

"I know," said Mrs. Weston. "I have spoken with her alone, but have not been able to break through the reserve. She admits that something is bothering her, but she will not say what."

"Is she well? She was complaining of fatigue."

"Possibly not. That could be the problem. If she is ill, it would be like her to hide it. Or at least that is what I believe she would have done if she were still poor and could not afford treatment. But she and Frank have plenty of money. Her behavior is a puzzle – an enigma."

"You are not the only ones in Highbury who have offered her a roof. We did, but she refused. I believe Mrs. Elton did too. Yet we all have very young children at home. Perhaps that is what is bothering her. Did she not--" and Emma lowered her voice, "—did she not have a miscarriage earlier?"

"I believe so," Mrs. Weston said, "but I never noticed any reluctance, any symptom of regret, when she plays with Anna."

"Then perhaps she is not well and she is afraid that being in a household with small children could tire her."

"Then why not return to Frank? He and his uncle are in London for the season. Their house has no small children and it has to be more comfortable than an apartment up two flights of stairs. Will you talk to her, Emma? If she is having difficulties with Frank, she may be reluctant to speak to me. I know the two of you were never close, but I also know I can rely on your discretion – I don't feel that I could confide in Mrs. Elton or Mrs. Cole."

Before Emma could reply, they were interrupted by a servant, bringing a note that had just been delivered. This action roused even Mr. Woodhouse, who had been drowsing in his chair.

"What is it?" asked Mr. Woodhouse, rather alarmed. "Who has sent the note?"

"It is from Mrs. Churchill," Emma answered.

"Ah, Mrs. Churchill," said Mr. Woodhouse, relaxing a little.

Mrs. Weston said nothing, but her glance was full of curiosity. Emma opened the letter, scanned it quickly, and then read aloud:

"Dear Mrs. Knightley,

"I wish to apologize for how ungrateful I must have appeared the other day, when you so kindly returned my grandmother's locket to me. Please forgive me. With my grandmother's death and my aunt's murder, I have not quite been myself.

"Of course I am grateful to have the locket back – it is a precious family heirloom – and in return for your efforts, I would like to make a gift to you of one of my grandmother's drawings. Given your interest in sketching yourself, I think you will appreciate it, even if you do prefer portraits of men and women to sketches of the local flora.

"Very cordially yours,

"Jane Fairfax Churchill."

Emma had to read the note twice to her father before he understood, but he was touched. "Very kind of her, very appropriate," he said. "You know that the Bates family cannot afford more, so a personal gift like this is really kind."

"I don't think Mrs. Churchill lacks funds," Emma said, "but I agree it is a kind gesture."

"What is the picture?" asked Mr. Woodhouse.

"It is a mushroom," said Emma, studying the rather faded sketch, and then showing it to him.

"A mushroom? It would be much prettier to have a drawing of a flower, I should think. Cowslips – or daisies."

"I have to agree with you, Papa," said Emma.

"Still, it is well done. I had forgotten how well Mrs. Bates drew! As do you, my dear," said the old man fondly.

"May I look at it too, Emma?" Mrs. Weston asked.

"Of course," Emma said, passing it to her friend, who took the paper to the window to study it in the sunlight.

"Very kind of Mrs. Churchill to send it to us," said Mr. Woodhouse. "Very attentive for her to give us a memento from Mrs. Bates. An old friend – I miss her. As I miss her daughter. But we are all getting on. Soon it will be time to bury me."

"Nonsense, Papa. Your health has been very good lately. You said so yourself at breakfast."

"Mr. Perry said he would call today – but he is not yet here. What do you suppose keeping him?"

Mrs. Weston walked back from the window and handed the sketch back to Emma. "Mrs. Bates was a talented artist – this is a very faithful depiction of *Amanita phalloides*."

Emma was planning to ask Mrs. Weston about the mushroom, when Mr. Woodhouse's long-awaited Mr. Perry was brought into the parlor. After the usual greetings, Mr. Perry apologized for his tardiness. "Mr. Woodhouse, there was a real emergency at the Gilbert farm – a sick child – a young girl."

"Oh, dear, a sick girl!" exclaimed Mr. Woodhouse. "I hope it is not serious. And one of the Gilbert girls, you say? A Miss Gilbert? Emma, do we know Miss Gilbert?"

"Not very well, Papa. Mr. Knightley knows the Gilberts, though – they are neighbors."

"Miss Gilbert is perfectly fine, sir," said Mr. Perry. "The patient is a younger girl – the daughter of a laborer – a Kizzy Draper."

"One of the Draper girls! Who sang at the Vicarage?" asked Mrs. Weston alertly.

Emma noticed a slump in Mr. Perry's shoulders. Her heart fluttering with fear, she asked, "Is Kizzy Draper all right, Mr. Perry?"

"No, she is not. Her condition is serious."

"Dear me," said Mr. Woodhouse, "how sad."

"What is the matter?" asked Mrs. Weston.

"She has a high fever and a putrid cough."

"But Mr. Gilbert said the Drapers had left," Emma objected.

"That's what they led everyone to believe," said Mr. Perry, "but they only pretended to depart. In truth, they were hiding in an old barn on the Gilbert farm – Mr. Gilbert was reluctant to lose his help during the harvest – and I think that caused the problem. It wasn't warm enough for the little girl, and during yesterday's storm she got wet."

"It is important to stay warm and dry," said Mr. Woodhouse.

"You are absolutely right, Papa," Emma agreed.

"Is the little girl – not Miss Gilbert – warm and dry now, Mr. Perry?"

Mr. Perry assured them that the little girl had been moved to a better room and that she was wrapped in warm dry blankets and was consuming hot broths – but he could not guarantee that she would recover. They all agreed that they were concerned, and then Mr. Perry accompanied Mr. Woodhouse into a different room in order to perform his usual examination.

"I must return to Randalls," said Mrs. Weston, gathering her daughter. "Do try to talk to Jane, if you can, Emma. I'm worried about her."

"I will go as soon as I can," said Emma, thinking that Jane would still probably not confide in her but that she might be very interested to learn that the Drapers had never left the parish of Donwell.

23 REVELATIONS

Again Emma walked to Highbury and to the building with the Bates apartment. As she opened the door, she gave a start, for she nearly bumped into Patty, the wiry gray-haired servant who had been with the Bateses for so many years.

"Mrs. Knightley!" Patty said "My apologies."

"How are you, Patty?" Emma asked.

"Well enough, Mrs. Knightley."

"Your future – will you be staying in Highbury? Or going with Mrs. Churchill?"

"So kind to ask! Mrs. Knightley, I don't know. Mrs. Churchill has asked me to stay with her for now, and she's been most generous – doubled my wages, she has."

"I'm sure no servant is more deserving," said Emma. "Is Mrs. Churchill at home? May I go upstairs?"

"Yes, Mrs. Knightley. Excuse me now, I have my errands."

And Patty headed in the direction of the post office, the task of retrieving letters having been resumed by her now that Jane Churchill was no longer carrying on a clandestine correspondence with a secret fiancé.

Emma opened the door and walked up the dark, narrow staircase; for once no conversation floated down towards her.

She knocked on the door; Mrs. Churchill opened it for her. "Oh! Mrs. Knightley – I was not expecting you."

"If my visit is inconvenient, I will leave at once."

"I did not mean to appear inhospitable. Please come in and sit down. I trust that you and your family are well? Even Mr. Woodhouse? Everything that is going on must upset him greatly."

Emma seated herself on a chair and assured Jane that her family was very well. "How are *you*, Mrs. Churchill?" she asked, studying the young woman's face, which was pale and even a little puffy. Jane did not appear ill, but she did not appear to be feeling well, either, and there were deep circles under her eyes.

"That is an excellent question, Mrs. Knightley. How am I? What should I tell you? What should I keep secret? You are correct, Mrs. Churchill; I am troubled."

"Without knowing more I cannot advise you, but if you wish to speak, I assure you that I would be discreet. And let me add that your friends are worried about you."

"I have promised to keep silent, but is it right to keep silent when you know of a wrong?"

Emma gazed at her with pity. She decided not to press Jane's reserve. "I came because there are a few specific items I wish to discuss. First, I want to tell you that Draper – you must have heard of him – is still in the area. He was hiding on the Gilbert farm."

Jane gained a little color at this piece of news, and hope flickered briefly in her eyes.

She *is* afraid, Emma thought. Mr. Knightley is right, she is terribly afraid.

"I don't think the Draper fellow has anything to do with me," Jane said. "I wish he was responsible for my aunt's death, but I don't think he is. Mrs. Knightley, *I* may be the cause, the inspiration, of so many wrongs. I cannot tell you, Mrs. Knightley, of what I have suffered."

Emma said, "Would you prefer that I ask questions?"

"It would be easier if another guessed the truth. If you guessed, I would not have to break my word."

It seemed an inefficient way to proceed, but Jane looked so distressed, and besides, there were many questions that Emma had long wished to pose to Jane. "It involves your husband?"

"Yes."

"Has he – has he betrayed you in some way?" Emma probed delicately, wondering if she was about to learn of a love affair that she had long suspected of Frank Churchill.

"Not exactly," said Jane, "but he has done far worse to others – or at least to one other, and all out of love for me. My dear Mrs. Knightley, I am absolutely wretched."

Jane's words poured water on Emma's first theory. A husband's infidelity would have to be considered a betrayal, and if Jane claimed that her husband had not betrayed her – not directly – then he had probably not had an affair.

"And you still love him?" Emma hazarded.

"Yes. But..."

"But you do not trust him."

"Not completely, no. How can I?"

Without more information – and it was frustrating because others, including the brilliant Jane Churchill, seemed to assume that she was cleverer than she was – Emma did not know how to answer this. She decided to pursue another point of curiosity. "Are you perfectly well, Jane?"

Jane did not answer.

Emma continued. "You have been exhausted. Your face is fuller. We are both matrons now, there is no shame – and you cannot expect to hide your condition for very long."

"You are right; I *am* expecting a child. But I was pregnant before, and lost the child, so you can understand why I have not wanted to confide in anyone about my situation. That is one of the reasons I have not accepted the invitations of my friends in Highbury."

"But your condition is just another reason for your not staying alone! You could fall ill – you could need assistance."

"Patty can assist me or call for assistance if there is a problem. She is here nearly all the time."

Emma nodded. "Of course. I'm sure Patty takes good care of you."

"She is a devoted servant."

Emma felt that she had received at least a partial answer regarding the mystery of Jane Churchill. "Very well," said Emma. She then took out the drawing by Mrs. Bates. "Why, Jane – I mean, Mrs. Churchill – why did you send me a sketch of a poisonous mushroom? Is it significant?"

Jane stared at her with a limpid, grey-eyed gaze. "Very."

"But what does that have to do with anything? Mrs. Bates, your grandmother, died of old age. Your aunt, Miss Bates, was hit over the head with a rock. Unless you sent it to me as a warning? Should *I* be afraid of *you?*"

"No – Mrs. Knightley – no, not at all. But someone did die of mushroom poisoning. Can you not think who?"

Emma frowned, thinking of all the deaths that had taken place in or around Highbury in the last twelvemonth, but none seemed to fit.

The door burst open, and Frank Churchill entered.

"Frank!" exclaimed Jane, at the sight of her husband.

Instead of the usual greetings, Frank Churchill addressed his wife in a voice that was low but angry. "You promised not to say anything! You gave me your word. But I have been listening to the conversation. You have broken your word, Jane!"

Emma recalled how often she had overheard conversations from the other side of this door – how she had eavesdropped on the Churchills themselves at the reception after the funeral of Mrs. Bates. In a way she deserved to be overheard, she thought, but she was still confused. "I do not understand what is going on," Emma said.

"Do not pretend ignorance, Mrs. Knightley," said Frank Churchill, his handsome face distorted by anger as he grabbed the poker from the fireplace. "You are quick to understand, and even if you do not comprehend everything yet, you soon would. You are a threat to my happiness."

Emma felt fear of a sort she had never known before. She backed away from him, unfortunately also away from the door, the only means of egress if she did not want to rush into another room and jump out of the window. She sat down on Mrs. Bates's old chair in the corner, while he waved the poker at her menacingly.

"Frank – Frank – if you do anything to Mrs. Knightley," Jane warned, coming to him and taking his arm, "if you harm her in any way, I will not live with you."

"You are not living with me now. I came back to Highbury to plead with you again, then found you having *this* conversation."

"If you harm Mrs. Knightley, I will never live with you."

His face relaxed, and he stepped away – but he was still between Emma and the door. "Jane, she is a danger to us."

"But what is going on? Why should he do anything to me? What is it he is supposed to have done? Oh! Mrs. Churchill!" said Emma, comprehending, and then added, more for her own benefit than for the sake of her listeners: "Your aunt, I mean, not your wife."

With all the swiftness of thought, Emma recalled how the old Mrs. Churchill had always been considered an obstacle to Frank Churchill's marriage to anyone – how that woman's famous pride, her influence over her easily guided husband, her jealous possessiveness of her husband's handsome young nephew, whom she had raised since he was a child of two – would have found fault with any young woman he might have chosen. This was even true of Jane Fairfax, who was beautiful, elegant, intelligent and accomplished – who had been raised by her father's friend Colonel Campbell in the best circles – but who came with no fortune and no noble connections, even though the origins of the other Mrs. Churchill were not illustrious either.

Emma also recalled how the first Mrs. Churchill had died when the secret engagement between Jane and Frank had been strained to the breaking point – how Jane had tried to end the relationship, and had made plans to go to a friend of Mrs. Elton's as a governess – how Mrs. Churchill's timely death had allowed Frank to come out in the open and pursue his courtship of Jane Fairfax without the secrecy that had troubled Jane so severely.

Frank said to his wife, "You see? She knows. She understands. And now we are in danger, and will be so long as she lives."

"As long as I live?" Emma asked, her terror increasing.

"What do you plan to do?" Jane demanded. "Would you kill Mrs. Knightley, too?"

A shiver ran through Emma as she stared at the Churchills.

"Your aunt at least was old and ailing," Jane reasoned, "and probably had only months, not years, to live. But Mrs. Knightley is young and healthy. She has a husband who loves her, a father who dotes on her, and a baby who needs her."

Frank hesitated, and sat down. "You are right, Jane, it is not the same."

Emma relaxed a little.

"What shall I do?" Frank asked. "What will we do?"

Jane said, most cautiously, most reasonably, "Mrs. Knightley has no *proof* of what happened. She only has suspicions."

"And my dear aunt has been buried for more than a year. If there was any sign in the body when she died, it has turned to dust long since." As Frank worked to persuade himself that Emma could do them no harm, that young matron wondered how she could escape. Should she scream? Run to the door?

Then Frank's reasoning seemed to go the other way. "I do not trust Mrs. Knightley. Even if she cannot prove the case against me, she can talk, and talk is enough to destroy my reputation, both in Highbury and with my uncle. I – *we* – will be ruined."

"What is the alternative?" asked Jane. "You cannot kill her without its being discovered.

"And how can I compel her to keep silent if I let her go? I have no hold over her. You at least love me, don't you, Jane?"

"Yes. It would be easier if I did not, but yes, Frank, I love you."

"Then promise to live with me again, and I will permit Mrs. Knightley to leave," said Frank.

Emma's eyes met Jane's, and in Jane's eyes she saw despair.

"Very well, Frank," said Jane, drawing herself up resolutely.

"Mrs. Knightley – Emma, whom I care for like a sister, whom I have no wish to harm – Jane will be safe with me as long as *you* remain silent. Do you understand?"

"I understand," Emma said.

"Then you may go," said Frank.

"Give me the poker, Frank," commanded Jane. "Mrs. Knightley will be reluctant to pass you if you still hold it."

Frank handed his wife the poker. Emma's knees quivered like custard, but she managed to rise from Mrs. Bates's old chair and cross the room slowly, each step feeling like a mile. She was still in danger, for Frank Churchill was strong enough to harm her even without the poker – but nevertheless she neared the door, and then she began to breathe more easily, because she was certain that she could open it and dash down the stairs before Frank caught up with her. But she was loath to leave Jane alone with Frank. Frank might love her, and Jane might love him, yet what sort of life could they have together?

Emma then said, "But what about Miss Bates? Mrs. Churchill – Jane – you cannot live with a man who killed your aunt!"

Frank shook his head. "I had nothing to do with the death of Miss Bates. I was not here; I was away in London with my uncle." Meeting her doubting look, he added: "I swear it! You may not believe me, but I swear it."

Emma looked at Jane; the other woman, still holding the poker nodded, confirming her husband's assertion.

"You mean Miss Bates *was* killed by gypsies? By that Draper fellow?" Emma asked, and swayed on her feet as she wondered if Highbury, her dear Highbury, was full of criminals born both high and low.

"No," Jane Churchill said, "my aunt was not killed by gypsies."

"But –" Emma began, and looked at Jane holding the poker, standing tall and strong and fierce despite her condition, perhaps because of it. "How can you speak with such assurance? Do you know who killed your aunt?" And she was certain that Jane did know, and if Jane had killed her aunt then she would have no doubt and little fear.

"Leave now, Mrs. Knightley," Jane commanded in a clear, hard voice. "Not all your questions will be answered."

Emma decided that Jane was right; it was better for some of her curiosity to remain unsatisfied, at least for the moment. She put her hand on the doorknob and started to open the door – and again had the odd sensation one has when another is pulling open the door at the same time one is pushing it.

In the shadows she saw a familiar figure. "Mr. Weston!" she exclaimed. "I am so glad to see you!"

"Emma," he said shortly, coming inside and pushing her back before him, so that she was once again in the middle of the apartment. He slammed the door behind him. "I should have known."

With the increased light of the apartment as opposed to the dark staircase, Emma could see that Mr. Weston was not smiling. Well, why should he be smiling? If he had heard any of the conversation transpiring in the Bates's apartment, he had to be suffering great disappointment in his son Frank, his pride and joy. And yet other words besides 'disappointment' occurred to her as better fitting the expression on his face: anger, sinister anger.

"My word! Mr. Weston, what is going on?" Emma cried out.

"You know too much," he said.

"I apparently know nothing," Emma said, "for I cannot understand your involvement in this."

"Then that is a pity," said Mr. Weston, and in his hand Emma saw his army pistol.

Emma wished just then that she were like her friend Harriet, who had the ability to faint in a situation such as this, for surely that would be better than what she was discovering: that dear Mr. Weston, the husband of her dearest friend, was turning out to be a monster! But she did not seem to be able to lose consciousness; instead her heart beat quicker than ever and she felt more intensely alive – just when she seemed most likely to be killed.

"You don't intend to use that on me," said Emma, horrified. "Surely you can't intend to use that on me."

"It may be old – from my army days – but I assure you it works," said Mr. Weston.

Jane, still holding the poker, moved forward and pushed Emma behind her. "And if I am not mistaken – Colonel Campbell taught me a little about artillery – that pistol contains only one bullet. You cannot kill both Mrs. Knightley and me."

"You know a lot, Jane – you know too much for a woman – but you do not know everything. It is possible to kill two people with one lucky shot, especially given how you are standing in front of Emma. And if they don't both die at once, then they will suffer horribly."

"Father, no!" said Frank.

"You would be better off without this Jane as your wife, Frank," Mr. Weston said. "I was willing to accept her and her lack of fortune – after all, I married Miss Taylor, also portionless and without connections. Money is not everything. But Jane does not want to live with you. She does not trust you. I am afraid she does not even love you. And she has failed to give you a child. Believe me, you would be happier with someone else. Next time, choose someone less discerning."

"Father, I love Jane. Put down your weapon."

"Frank, I wish I could," Mr. Weston said, but instead he aimed his pistol at his daughter-in-law and cocked it.

"No!" Frank cried, leaping forward, pushing the women out of the way - at the same time as there was a deafening bang. The women both screamed, and Emma tumbled to the floor, while Jane and Frank went sprawling as well.

Now it was Mr. Weston's to cry, "No!" in despair. He knelt beside Frank, who was bleeding in the chest.

Jane was the first to recover. She scrambled to her feet, and stood with the poker over Mr. Weston and his son. "You have shot him," she said coldly. "You shot your own son."

"Frank, I am so sorry," said Mr. Weston, taking his son's hand. "Frank, you will be all right."

"No – no I won't," the younger man gasped.

"Mrs. Knightley – Emma – are you all right?" Jane asked.

Emma pulled herself to her feet. Her lip was bleeding, for she had hit it on a table, but other than that she was uninjured. "Yes," she said.

"Then fetch help," Jane said. "Please."

"Of course," Emma said, and went once more to the door of the apartment. She opened it, to discover people rushing up the stairs.

"What is going on?" asked Patty, breathless.

"That was a pistol shot, that was," said Charles, the baker's boy who helped downstairs.

Patty entered the apartment, saw Frank Churchill groaning and bleeding on the rug on the floor, and screamed.

"There has been a terrible accident," Emma said, feeling as if her wits were returning to her at last. "Send someone for Mr. Perry. And send someone else to my husband. He should be at a meeting at the Crown."

"Yes, Mrs. Knightley," said Charlie, taking one last look into the apartment, then turning and clattering down the stairs.

"Thank you," Jane said to Emma, then she addressed her ash-faced servant. "Patty, fetch some linens."

"Yes, mum," said Patty, and put down her basket and darted into another room.

"Jane," Frank groaned from his position on the floor, "Jane, can you forgive me?"

Emma thought that Frank ought to be asking *her* for forgiveness, or for forgiveness from his dead, poisoned aunt, or even his uncle, her bereaved husband, but to Frank, Jane's affection and approval were all that mattered.

"Take this," Jane said to Emma, handing her the poker. "Move aside, Mr. Weston – my husband needs me." And she knelt beside the young man.

Emma was ready to wield the poker if Mr. Weston attempted to attack her again, but the older man did not. Instead he allowed his daughter-in-law to kneel by her husband, while remaining on the floor himself, cradling his son's head in his lap. Patty rushed back into the room and handed towels and bed linens to her mistress.

Jane pressed a towel against her husband's wound; the white cloth was soon stained with crimson.

"You'll be all right, son," he said. "They've sent for Mr. Perry."

"No, Father, I won't," said Frank. "I'm dying. Jane, please, tell me you forgive me."

"As a Christian, I forgive you," she said.

"You were always better than I. I never deserved you," said Frank. "But did I ever make you happy?"

"Oh, Frank!" Jane exclaimed, and finally the reserve broke down. "Of course – of course you did."

Emma heard footsteps running up the stairs. "Emma! Emma, are you all right?"

Mr. Knightley burst into the room, followed by spry Mr. Perry, Mr. Elton, Charlie the baker's boy and finally a puffing, red-faced Mr. Cole.

"Emma, my love, what is going on?" Mr. Knightley asked, while Mr. Perry pushed his way to Frank and knelt by the bleeding young man.

"Mr. Weston shot his son," Emma said, putting down the poker, and leaning against her husband's strong arm.

"What?" exclaimed Mr. Knightley. "An accident?"

"Not exactly," Emma replied. "I will explain everything to you in detail later, but Mr. Weston was trying to kill us – Mrs. Churchill and me – but he shot Frank instead."

Mr. Knightley, surveying the scene, gave a brief nod. Instead of asking further questions, he first told Mr. Elton to pick Mr. Weston's pistol up from the floor. Then Mr. Knightley compelled everyone to step back a little from the principals: Frank, lying on the floor, tended by the apothecary Mr. Perry, Frank's wife Jane, and Mr. Weston, Frank's father.

Tears ran down Mr. Weston's face. "I have done terrible things," he said. "But before you punish me – and I deserve punishment – can you help Frank? Perry, can you help Frank?"

"This wound is too severe," said Perry, pressing a fresh linen against it, and watching the blood spill out anyway. "I'm sorry."

"Will die," Frank gasped. "Hurts."

"Can you give him something for the pain?" demanded Mr. Weston.

"No," said Perry. "I am afraid he won't last long enough for laudanum drops to make a difference. There is no point in moving him, either – that would only cause him unnecessary pain."

Mr. Knightley inspected Emma's cut lip, and said that it would swell for a few days, but it did not look serious. She gripped his arm as they moved to the sofa and sat down. The minutes they spent in the Bates apartment were few, but they were imbued with an intensity that created memories starker than any Emma had ever known. The sight of those on the floor: Frank, surrounded by his father and his wife. Frank's labored breathing. The blood at the corner of his mouth, a sign that the internal injury was too great. The wheezing breaths of Mr. Cole, who seated himself by the piano. The serious expressions on the men's faces. The smell of the many people in the small parlor, the smell of gunpowder and the smell of Frank Churchill's blood. The throbbing of her lip. Mr. Knightley's arm around her, and Emma's gratitude that her husband was a truly good man who deserved her confidence and trust.

Mr. Elton recalled that he was a clergyman and gave the gun to Mr. Cole and administered extreme unction.

"He is dead," Perry announced.

"My dear boy! My beloved son!" said Mr. Weston, and he closed Frank Churchill's unseeing eyes. Then he tenderly moved Frank's head from his lap to a cushion on the floor, and stiffly rose to his feet. "Mr. Knightley and Mr. Cole, I am implicated in four deaths—" everyone gasped at this number, and even Emma, counting rapidly, could not identify all the victims, "—and so I give myself over to you. As Jane has every reason to want me out of her sight, I suggest that you escort me to the Crown Inn and put me under guard there. Mr. and Mrs. Stokes are best equipped for dealing with this situation and are not as deeply involved and so will be less distressed. Jane – Emma – I apologize for my behavior."

Emma could not help observing that Mr. Weston, now that the crisis was over, had reverted to his usual obliging and considerate personality, even giving advice on how to arrest him while causing the least fuss to others.

"Very well," said Mr. Knightley, and after a quick word with Emma, he, Cole and Elton took Mr. Weston away.

.

24 A MURDERER'S CONFESSION

Emma remained with Jane a little longer in the apartment.

"Can I help you? Is there anything you need?"

Mrs. Churchill, still kneeling by the body of her dead husband, said that she was grateful for Mrs. Knightley's offer, but that she would be all right. "I am not alone. Mr. Perry knows what must be done, and Patty is with me."

Emma put on her coat and walked to the door again. This time her passage was not blocked; this time no one burst through it to threaten her and Jane. She paused on the threshold to say, "Thank you for saving my life, Mrs. Churchill."

"Mrs. Knightley, if not for me you would have never been in danger," Jane replied.

Emma then descended the staircase, thinking of all the things she had to do. First and foremost – Mrs. Weston needed to be informed. Poor Mrs. Weston! Mr. Woodhouse had always described her as poor since her marriage to Mr. Weston, but for the first time the epithet seemed just. Her father, it turned out, was in his way prescient. It occurred to her then that Mr. Knightley would send someone to inform Mrs. Weston, or might even go himself, and that as dear as Mrs. Weston was and as great as her claims might be, Emma's first duty was to her father. She had an overwhelming desire to reach the safety of Hartfield, jumping a little as a dog barked and as a pair of boys ran past. She felt deeply relieved as she crossed through the iron sweep-gate and entered her own property.

The vestibule was rather dark, so the butler did not notice anything wrong as he took her coat – simply informing her that the baby had just settled down for his nap. When she entered the parlor, concerned for her father, she found him asleep in his chair before the fire, completely unaware of the terrible events. Emma alone and finally safe, indulged in some private tears. When the maid arrived with the tea cart, only then did anyone notice Emma's tears and her swollen lip.

"Madam! Oh, my word, Madam! Are you all right?"

"Some dreadful things have happened, but I do not have the strength to explain. You will learn everything soon enough. As for my lip, I fell and cut it on a table. Bring me something to clean it with, will you, Maggie?"

The maid rushed to comply, while Emma poured herself some tea – which proved to be awkward and even a little painful to drink with her bruised lip. But the warm liquid was comforting in its way.

So many questions remained. Mr. Weston had mentioned that he had been instrumental in *four* deaths. Which four? Frank Churchill, obviously. Miss Bates. The first Mrs. Churchill. But who else?

The maid returned and helped Emma tend her lip. They were about this when Mr. Woodhouse awoke from his doze before the fire. He was alarmed to find that his dear daughter had been injured and wanted to send for Mr. Perry immediately. Emma, aware that the apothecary had more significant cases to tend to, made light of her situation.

"What happened? How could you have hurt your lip so?"

Emma explained that she had slipped and fallen.

"You should not be outside walking about. There is mud, after such a storm as we had, there is certainly mud. You should take better care of yourself, my dear Emma; you are too delicate for such adventures. Let James drive you, or if you walk, take Mr. Knightley with you so that you can hold on to his arm."

Emma was in no mood to argue this point. "Yes, Papa."

"Where exactly did you fall? Near the Crown Inn – in front of Ford's?"

"No, Papa. I was at the Bates apartment."

"You fell inside? On the stairs, perhaps? I remember that they have a dangerous staircase."

"No, Papa. Papa, you must prepare yourself. There has been a terrible accident."

Emma was reluctant to tell her father what had happened, because it would overburden him, yet it was impossible to keep this information away from him. Best that he hear it from her, when he could see that she was alive and relatively safe, if not completely uninjured.

Mr. Woodhouse was absolutely horrified. Frank Churchill dead! Shot by his own father, their dear Mr. Weston! In front of Emma! Had Emma been shot? Was she certain that the injury to her lip was not a gunshot?

Emma could not speak lightly of such grave matters but she did her best to reassure her father that she was well. She promised to see Mr. Perry when he was available, and represented that others needed the apothecary's care more than she did.

"Who?" demanded Mr. Woodhouse who could not admit that others' claims might be more pressing than his daughter's.

"Mrs. Jane Churchill, who saw her husband die. Mr. Weston, who must be horrified that he killed his son. Mrs. Weston – Papa, you know how sensitive Mrs. Weston is. She must be reeling from shock. If Mr. Perry can help her in this situation, we must let him do so."

Mr. Woodhouse had trouble acknowledging the superiority of the claims of the widow and the bereaved father, but Mrs. Weston – their own dear Mrs. Weston, who had lived at Hartfield for so many years – he agreed that Mr. Perry should tend her if she needed it. Emma did not explain how much Mrs. Weston might need assistance – she wished she could go to her friend just then.

"And where is Mr. Knightley?" asked Mr. Woodhouse fretfully. "Why is he not home, taking care of us?"

"He has things to do, Papa," said Emma, although she wondered that point herself. "We are perfectly safe."

Mr. Woodhouse was of the opinion that if Mr. Weston could start shooting people in apartments, then no place was safe. Emma did what she could to soothe him, but it was hard work, especially as part of her agreed with her father. The two of them ate supper – a note arriving from Mr. Knightley that he was detained – and the minutes ticked by. Finally, after the baby had fallen asleep and even Mr. Woodhouse, despite the day's excitement, had begun to yawn, Mr. Knightley arrived from the Crown Inn. He kissed his wife and baby, assured his father-in-law that he was well, that Frank Churchill was definitely dead – and that Mr. Weston, who had been so dear to them for many years but had turned out to be a dangerous murderer – that Mr. Weston would die.

Mr. Woodhouse and his daughter exclaimed in astonishment.

"What? Is he to be hanged?" Mr. Woodhouse demanded.

"How could that be decided so quickly?" asked Emma. "No, of course it has not. Did he have a second pistol? Has he shot himself?"

Mr. Knightley explained that they were both wrong. It turned out that Mr. Weston had had some of the poisonous mushroom about him. They had searched him for additional weapons, but left him with what they thought was simply a snuff box – they thought it would be kind to leave it with him – and it had contained some of the mushroom that he had given to his son to poison Mrs. Churchill. Mr. Weston had consumed it, a lethal dose.

"What about Mr. Perry?" Emma demanded. "Can he do anything for Mr. Weston?"

Mr. Perry had seen him and confirmed that there was no antidote. Mr. Weston would suffer for a while, then seem to recover for about half a day – and then he would die, unless some miracle intervened.

Emma and her father both expressed their horror. Then Emma inquired after Mrs. Weston.

"She has been taken to see him. And Mr. Weston has asked to see you, too, Emma. I have come to see if I can escort you to the Crown Inn."

"Me?" asked Emma.

Mr. Woodhouse was appalled at the idea of his daughter going to visit a murderer. "Especially so late at night!"

"I assure you, sir, I will protect Emma," Mr. Knightley said.

"But why does he want to see me?" Emma asked.

"I think he wishes to apologize for what he has done, and to ask forgiveness. Will you come? You need have no fear. And if you do not come now – well, very soon, it will be too late."

Emma considered quickly. Mr. Weston was obviously not the man she had always taken him to be, yet despite what had transpired she could not so easily hate a man she had always looked upon as a friend. For so many years he had been a favorite! Was it all a lie? And then she thought of her dear friend Mrs. Weston. Even if she were not to go for *his* sake, she would have to go for *hers*.

"Very well," said Emma, feeling that she could hardly refuse a deathbed request. "Papa, I will be safe with Mr. Knightley – you know I will be safe."

"But who will protect me?" Mr. Woodhouse fretted.

They assigned that responsibility to the coachman and to the butler, and then Mr. and Mrs. Knightley went out into the night. The distance to the Crown Inn was not far, and as long as one wore sensible boots instead of dancing slippers, the walk was easy. During it Emma experienced many peculiar sensations: what could a dying murderer want to say to *her*? How could she be so important as to warrant being asked to his deathbed?

When they reached the Crown Inn, however, she discovered she was not the only person that Mr. Weston had asked to visit him before he died. As she was escorted to another room in which she could wait, she learned that Mr. William Cox, the lawyer, was with him. Well, Mr. Weston had been a man of business; it was natural for him to want to set things in order before he died.

But others were gathered as well; it seemed like a large number, and Emma could not help thinking that Mr. Weston had always been friendly with many, and that to be the favorite and intimate of a man who had so many intimates and confidantes, was not the very first distinction in the scale of vanity. Yet when she looked at the crowd which had gathered, she could understand why most had come. The Eltons were there – Mr. Elton in his official capacity, as he would be expected to give Mr. Weston extreme unction, and Mrs. Elton's words made it clear that she would never sit at home alone on an occasion such as this, insisting that she needed to be there to lend support to her *caro sposo*. Perhaps she *was* succoring him; who could tell? Even Mr. Elton, whose hypocrisy ran deep, might find it difficult to minister to a man and neighbor who turned out to be a murderer. Next to Mrs. Elton sat Jane Churchill, her face white and her expression solemn – now *her* presence, given that Mr. Weston had tried to kill her, and given that he had caused the death of her husband, was more difficult to comprehend. *She* did not appear to be here in order to gratify either curiosity or vanity; her expression of dignified disgust made it clear that she had only come because she thought it was the right thing to do.

Emma scanned the room for Mrs. Weston, but Mrs. Elton informed her that Mrs. Weston was with her husband and the lawyer. Emma and her husband took seats, and then Mr. Perry – it was easy to understand why Highbury's apothecary was here, even if he could not hope to cure Mr. Weston, he might be able to alleviate his suffering – Mr. Perry came over to her and inquired after herself and her father. "I have not had time to look at your lip, or to see if you are suffering from the shock of this morning."

Emma assured the apothecary that her hurt was superficial, and although she was still horrified and saddened by the events of this terrible day, *she* was all right. As for her father, he was very distressed, but he had retired for the night. "Thank you so much for the sleeping draught. I am sure he will sleep the night through. He always does."

"I'm glad to hear it," said Mr. Perry.

"Perry, have you any idea when Weston will want to see Mrs. Knightley?" Mr. Knightley asked.

Mr. Perry, however, knew little more than the others in the room. Mr. Knightley brought Emma a cup of tea from a pot that Mrs. Stokes had placed on the sideboard, and she settled down for a long wait. Most were quiet, even Mrs. Elton. Glancing at Mr. Elton, Emma recalled how embarrassed she had once felt in his presence, after he proposed marriage to her. That shame, which at the time had seemed so deep, so dreadful, was only a shallow memory now. Especially compared to what Jane Churchill and Mrs. Weston must be experiencing!

Even on his deathbed Mr. Weston was practical; twenty minutes later, Mr. Cox came into the room and asked for Mrs. Knightley and Mrs. Churchill. Emma squeezed her husband's hand; "I should like Mr. Knightley to come with me."

"By all means."

The Knightleys rose from their chairs, but most eyes were focused on Jane Churchill. Would she go to see the murderer of her husband?

Mrs. Churchill stood. Mr. Cox offered her his arm, and they made a strange procession, the lawyer and the widow; followed by the Knightleys. Emma's heart seemed to leap in all sorts of strange directions inside her; what would they find?

They went to a room that was used by visitors to Highbury. Mr. Weston was inside it - not on a bed, but stretched out upon a sofa, his face rather gray. He was not tied to anything, and Mrs. Weston sat on a chair beside the sofa, holding his hand. Her eyes were wet and red, but she was calm.

"Thank you for coming," said Mr. Weston, and Emma was surprised to hear how normal and ordinary his voice sounded, as if he was the same Mr. Weston who had always been so welcomed by her family and her friend – and she supposed he was the same Mr. Weston, but that she had never known him completely. "Both of you. Please, sit down."

Emma took a seat on the other side of Mrs. Weston, and Mr. Knightley sat beside her. Jane, however, remained standing.

"What do you have to say?" asked Jane, and her voice shook a little, but her posture was straight.

"I want to ask you both for forgiveness. I am a murderer, but I am about to die, and so before I do I want to tell you what happened."

Mrs. Weston shook her head slightly, as if she could not bear to hear everything again, and Emma squeezed her hand. Jane said nothing and so Mr. Knightley cleared his throat and asked Mr. Weston to continue.

"Yes, I know I do not have much time. It started long ago. When I was a boy, Jane, wandering around the fields and woods near Highbury, your grandmother took me and several other children and explained which mushrooms were safe to eat – and which would kill you – and how. The other children included your mother and your aunt."

"And?"

"I wondered if your aunt recalled that conversation. I was frightened – not so much for myself, Jane, but for those I loved – love more than myself. My wife, our daughter Anna, and especially my son Frank."

"But now your son is dead," Emma could not help saying.

"Yes – and he gave his life to save you and Jane."

"Continue about the mushrooms," Mrs. Weston said.

"Yes, my dear. Do you remember that day more than a year ago, when we went to Box Hill? I knew something was bothering Frank. He would not tell me what – he respected the secrecy of your engagement, Jane – but I guessed that Mrs. Churchill was thwarting his life's plans. While we were exploring, I found some of those mushrooms. I gave them to him and explained what they could do.

"Obviously it was wrong of me – and of Frank – to use the mushrooms on Mrs. Churchill. But according to him, she was ill and suffering, and would not live much longer anyway."

"If Mrs. Churchill was dying, then why did you kill her?" Jane asked.

"Frank was terribly distressed – as I said – and Mrs. Churchill had been complaining of illness for years. She might have lasted for years, and destroyed all his hopes of happiness. Yes, Jane, I see the mistake in my reasoning – you may add hypocrisy to my many sins! I told myself that she was about to die but if I had truly believed that I would not have acted as I did."

They fell silent, contemplating this admission of murder. Then Emma asked, because she felt the question needed to be asked, and she was not sure if Jane could ask it. "And Miss Bates?"

"After Mrs. Bates died – and I did not kill her; her death was natural – Miss Bates was the only one in Highbury who knew about my connection to the deadly mushrooms in the past. You were staying with her, Jane – and you were clever. I knew how much Frank loved you, and I wanted to make sure you learned nothing from your aunt. So after the concert at the Eltons, when I realized I could meet with Miss Bates alone, I first went home and then told my wife that I was working on important papers and was not to be disturbed. Then I left through the window of my study, went back to the graveyard, and waited for Miss Bates there."

"Where you killed her," said Mr. Knightley.

"Yes, I killed her, but I made sure I struck her very hard, so that she suffered as little as possible," said Mr. Weston. "Yes, I am aware how self-serving I sound – how terribly I have acted. But I want to assure you, Jane, that she fell after a single blow and stopped breathing almost immediately. And then I took her locket, so that it would look as if she were robbed. The gypsies would be blamed. But then Emma found the locket, and Jane – who already had her suspicions about Mrs. Churchill's death – sent Emma Mrs. Bates's sketch of the death-cap mushroom."

"You wanted innocent people to be suspected in Miss Bates's death?" asked the fair-minded Mr. Knightley, more furious than Emma had ever heard him.

Mr. Weston sighed. "I was desperate to protect Frank – and my relationship with Frank. I could not have used mushrooms again; he would have realized what I had done, and even Miss Bates – or you, Jane – might have understood that she was being killed by the death cap. Besides, Miss Bates suffered far less from the blow to the head than she would have if I had poisoned her."

"But those innocent people! To be falsely accused! Perhaps they are accustomed to it, but does that not make it worse?" asked Emma, horrified.

Mrs. Weston finally spoke. "Emma, Mr. Weston has asked Mr. Cox to make sure the fellow receives fifty pounds in reparation."

Mr. Knightley nodded grudgingly. "That is a start."

"Given my situation, it is all that I can do," said Mr. Weston.

Jane, still standing, spoke. "Mr. Weston, did you ever use those mushrooms any other time?"

Mr. Weston sighed.

"Well? Did you?" Mr. Knightley repeated Jane's question.

Emma watched as Mr. Weston nodded, and listened with horror as he continued to confess. "My wife – my first wife, Frank's mother – also suffered from a long illness. She was spending freely, taking away from what should have been Frank's fortune. As the apothecary told me her condition was hopeless, anyway, it did not seem so very wrong."

Jane said, "So, in effect, you killed both of Frank's mothers – and my aunt – and you would have killed me."

At this summary – with the inclusion of Frank the tally became four – Emma recoiled. "A wife killer!" she could not help saying. Even Mrs. Weston shuddered.

"Yes, I have been a wicked man, and I tempted Frank into wickedness as well. I should have been patient; I should have counseled Frank to be patient."

He coughed, and beads of sweat broke out on his forehead. "I do not have long to live, and I deserve to die. I ask nothing for myself. But those I love – my wife and my little daughter – I ask you, Emma, and you, Jane to help. Not financially – I have settled my affairs with Mr. Cox, and Mr. John Knightley has my will – but forgive them."

Emma was moved despite herself. "You can be sure that I will always treat Mrs. Weston as my dearest friend."

Jane Churchill was a little cooler, but her losses had been far greater than Emma's. "You may rest assured that I bear Mrs. Weston and your daughter no ill will."

Mr. Weston nodded.

"Is there anything else?"

"No – " he said, and his face was turning grey, "—send Perry to me."

Mr. Knightley escorted Emma and Jane from the room.

25 CONFIDANTES AT LAST

Despite no one at Hartfield besides Mr. Woodhouse and little George Knightley having slept well, the next morning Emma rose early. A note arrived from Mrs. Weston that Mr. Weston had died during the night, and that, although she knew she would need condolence later, that day she preferred to be alone at Randalls.

Mr. Woodhouse spent the morning shaking his head and exclaiming over the events. "Mr. Weston! Mr. Weston killed so many people!"

"Yes, sir," said Mr. Knightley, who had decided to stay at Hartfield that day, supporting his wife after her ordeal.

"Poor Mrs. Weston! What will she do?"

"We will visit her later, Papa," said Emma. "Today she asked to be alone, but later she will need us."

That day, Emma had no desire to leave Hartfield. Most of Highbury's gentlewomen seemed to prefer the safety of their own hearths – even though the murderers were dead – and most made it clear that their husbands should stay home as well. One exception was Mr. Perry, who looked as if he wanted sleep himself, but who called to see how they all were. He informed them that the bodies of Mr. Weston and his son had been moved to the undertaker and Mr. Elton was consulting with their widows about funerals. On a more cheerful note he reported that the little Draper girl was recovering.

"I am glad to hear it," Emma said. "Now you should go home and rest."

"Yes, my friend, take care of yourself, or who else will take care of us?" said Mr. Woodhouse.

Yawning, Mr. Perry departed from Hartfield to go home and take a nap.

At Hartfield the inmates relaxed. The baby turned over for the first time from his stomach to his back, and enjoyed the applause and smiles of his parents so much that he tried to do it again. Mr. Woodhouse talked about his gruel; Mr. Knightley wrote letters of business about the Donwell harvest, and Emma chatted with the three men in her family.

In the afternoon, to Emma's great surprise, Mrs. Churchill called at Hartfield.

After greeting them all, and mutually satisfying themselves regarding each other's health, Mrs. Churchill asked if she could speak in private with Mrs. Knightley.

"Of course," Emma said, rising.

Mr. Knightley stayed with Mr. Woodhouse, working on his correspondence at the desk but also commiserating with his father-in-law when Mr. Woodhouse required it, which allowed Emma to lead Jane Churchill into the small parlor and offer her a seat.

"I hope it is not too cold in here," Emma said, and told a housemaid to bring them tea and to stoke the fire. When these things were done, and they were finally alone, she asked: "How are you really, Mrs. Churchill?"

Mrs. Churchill smiled wryly at her hostess. "I still don't know. I have not yet decided. But there is one thing I am certain of, Mrs. Knightley – I owe you an apology. I involved you in a dangerous situation, and you could have been hurt or killed. I wish there was some way I could compensate for this."

Emma poured tea for them both. It was strange to think that Jane Churchill could feel as guilty about her as she had ever felt about Jane Churchill. She decided to press her advantage. "I understand you were sworn to secrecy before, but if you could let me know what happened..."

"Of course," Jane said, then asked a question Emma did not expect. "Have you studied mathematics?"

"Mathematics! No, of course not," said Emma.

"I have. These days great progress is being done in understanding what is likely and what is not."

"Through mathematics?" Emma asked, thinking that no matter how well she thought she knew the citizens of Highbury, discoveries could always be made. Mrs. Bates was a naturalist; her granddaughter a mathematician. And only yesterday she had learned that Mr. Weston and his son were killers.

Jane continued. "When Mrs. Churchill died – the previous Mrs. Churchill, my husband Frank's aunt – at the time I felt nothing but relief at the bounty of God. It may have been wrong of me to rejoice in the death of a fellow human being, but I had heard that she was ill, and that she was suffering, and I felt she spread nothing but unhappiness. But later..."

"Yes?"

"Later it struck me that the timing was *too* convenient. And Mr. Churchill – Frank's uncle – told me that his wife, although her health had been deteriorating for some time, for years in fact – Mrs. Churchill died of a seizure of a completely different nature."

"Ah!" said Emma, comprehending, at least in part. "And you became suspicious. When did you realize that it was mushrooms?"

"I asked Mr. Churchill to describe how she died and her symptoms were exactly those that someone who consumed poisonous mushrooms – the death cap with the white spots – would experience. And I remembered that my aunt had shown me some on Box Hill when we explored there." She shook her head. "Many have assumed that I would be a good influence on Frank. And I believe I was, in certain respects. But he was always tempted to short cuts, to taking the easy way instead of doing what was strictly right."

"His affection for you was genuine," said Emma.

"I believe it was. Yet when I became convinced that something was – wrong – about Mrs. Churchill's death, *I* no longer felt comfortable around him. He noticed my distancing myself. At first he thought it was because I was upset because I had had a miscarriage, but in truth it was because I suspected – and later became convinced – that I was married to a murderer."

"Were you frightened?" asked Emma.

"Of course! I did not know what to do. I would have left – I considered going to the Campbells, but they were in Ireland. I even considered going out to be a governess, as I had once planned, but then I discovered I was with child. But when my grandmother died, it gave me the excuse to spend some time away from Frank."

"Did he know why you wanted to be apart?"

"Yes. Frank was clever. He discovered that I had corresponded with my aunt about poisonous mushrooms – and he realized that I had spoken to his uncle about Mrs. Churchill's death. Frank knew that I knew, and begged me not to tell anyone what he had done. I promised I would not, in exchange for him letting me stay in Highbury."

"With your aunt."

"Yes, in my aunt's apartment, even though more comfortable alternatives were available to me. As you know, I am with child. Because my child's father is a murderer, I was finding it difficult to rejoice in the fact and so I did not want to tell anyone about it. I was sure that if I stayed with you, or the Westons – or even the Eltons – my secret would be discovered. But as you know, being with child is exhausting. On the day of Mrs. Elton's musical afternoon I really did want to sleep. So I stayed home, but my aunt never came back."

"Did you suspect--?"

"Mrs. Knightley, I honestly did not know what to think. Frank was supposed to be in London with his uncle, and although the distance is not insurmountable, it seemed unlikely. How would he know that my aunt was in the graveyard? And yet, as I knew that he had murdered *his* aunt, I could not help wondering if he had murdered *mine*."

"The locket," Emma said.

"Yes, the locket. The locket – the possibility that my aunt had been killed for gold – that was comforting. And yet there were difficulties. I know that Donwell Abbey had been robbed, but no one here has been harmed before."

"Did you suspect Mr. Weston?"

"I did. If Frank had any accomplice in Highbury, who other than his father? I determined that Mr. Weston could have done it – and when you gave me my grandmother's locket, I believed he had done it."

"But when did he hide the locket at the beech tree?"

"Did he not go with Mr. Knightley to question that fellow at the Gilbert estate?"

"Yes," Emma said. "Mr. Weston must have hidden it then, or on his way home, because Mr. Knightley remained a while afterwards at Donwell Abbey."

"Ah – I thought it must have been something like that."

Emma poured them each another cup of tea. "I can hardly imagine how trapped you must have felt."

"I was desperate. I knew Frank had killed his aunt – but I had promised not to tell anyone about it. You were the only one in Highbury who I thought was clever enough and suspicious enough to figure out the truth, so I sent you my grandmother's drawing of the mushroom."

Emma was flattered to be deemed clever by the educated and accomplished Jane Churchill, who spoke so casually of 'mathematics.' "I knew something was wrong – even Mrs. Weston knew something was wrong – but I did not understand what."

"Poor Mrs. Weston! I believe she is innocent in all this."

"I am sure of it, Mrs. Churchill."

"Please, call me Jane. Mrs. Churchill is the name of a woman who was murdered by my husband. I would prefer that you called me Jane."

"You may call me Emma," said Emma.

26 TWO MORE FUNERALS

Mr. Elton conducted two more funerals in Highbury, burying Mr. Weston and his son in the local family plot. As both were confessed murderers, it was done rather hastily, to avoid any discussion about the propriety of keeping their earthly remains in the Highbury parish. But Mr. Elton armored himself with the defense that he had administered extreme unction to each – and both had been so popular while they lived – but rather to his surprise, and Mrs. Elton's, no one objected.

For the women of Highbury, there had been many changes. Old Mrs. Bates was dead, but that was hardly a surprise. Poor Miss Bates was murdered. Mrs. Weston was alive, but now ashamed of her husband and almost relieved that he was dead. Mrs. Jane Churchill was packing her aunt's and grandmother's things, and preparing to leave Highbury.

Emma, who only a few weeks ago had felt like the least-liked gentlewoman in Highbury, was suddenly very popular. Mrs. Cole, Mrs. Perry, and even Mrs. Elton, curious to learn exactly what had transpired in the Bates apartment, called at Hartfield to learn everything they could. And Mrs. Churchill – Jane – visited as well and let Emma know what was happening and her plans for the future.

Jane told Emma that she had written an explanation of everything to Frank's uncle Mr. Churchill, who was horrified to learn that his wife had been murdered. The events were so significant that he came down to Highbury to see his nephew's grave – staying in the best room at the Crown Inn – and met with both Mrs. Weston and Mrs. Churchill. One point that Jane related was rather illuminating. Mr. Churchill claimed that Mrs. Churchill – the deceased Mrs. Churchill – had never trusted Mr. Weston. "Handsome, charming, but weak," were the words that Mrs. Churchill had used to describe him. "It seems she was right," Mr. Churchill continued.

"My wife was a good judge of character. We tried to bring Frank up to be better, but could not overcome his natural defects."

Mr. Churchill was pleased to learn Jane was expecting, and hoped that the child would prove more resolute than its father and grandfather. He settled a sum on Jane Churchill, who announced that she would leave England to visit her friends in Ireland. She departed from Highbury, taking her faithful servant Patty with her.

Mr. Knightley's harvest was in, so he only went several days each week to Donwell, and could spend more time at Hartfield. The day that Mr. Weston and his son were buried, he said to Emma of Frank Churchill: "You always called him the child of good fortune. It seems he played a role in making his own good fortune."

"Yes," Emma sighed. "Too large a role." Then she asked Mr. Knightley if he knew how Harriet was doing.

With all the excitement, Emma had nearly forgotten Harriet and her suffering, but now she had an idea. She went with Mr. Knightley one crisp day to Donwell Abbey, where she finally saw the cider press, then went a little further in the carriage to call on the Gilberts. After a discussion with Mrs. Gilbert, and later with Noah Draper and his daughters, she arranged for the older girl, Florica, to train as a maid at the Martins. With the girl's assistance, Harriet recovered her looks and spirits, and the next time Emma called she was able to tell Emma that the people who had frightened her that day at the back gate were none other than the two Draper girls. They had been sent by their father in search of Mr. Gilbert's escaped bull calf. The girls, too, had noticed earlier that someone had been making trips through the side door of Donwell Abbey, but their father had forbidden them to say anything, simply because he did not want them involved.

Later Mr. Knightley asked, "How is your friend, Mrs. Weston?"

"She is avoiding me," said Emma, sighing. "I think she feels guilty because *she* told Mr. Weston that Jane had sent me the drawing by Mrs. Bates – the sketch of the poisonous mushroom – which is what prompted him to go the Bates apartment with his pistol."

"But it is not her fault – she had no idea!"

"I know that. I believe she knows that. But she cannot forgive herself."

Mr. Knightley scratched his chin. "I will talk to her and tell her how much she is missed at Hartfield."

"Would you?" asked Emma. "Not only I miss her, but my father misses her. And Baby George is in love with her daughter."

Mr. Knightley called on Mrs. Weston, and the next day she resumed her calls at Hartfield, but the visits were awkward, and Emma wondered if they would ever be at ease with each other again.

147

27 RESTORED TREASURE

They were sitting in the parlor just after dinner – Mr. Woodhouse asleep before the fire, the baby asleep as well, Mr. Knightley reading aloud to Emma as she attempted to sketch her father – she was not satisfied with her efforts and wondered if, like old Mrs. Bates, she should concentrate on drawing flora and fungi.

They heard a carriage pulling into the drive. "Who could that be?" asked Mr. Knightley, putting down his book, and even Mr. Woodhouse was roused from his doze.

It was Mr. John Knightley, arrived from London. His appearance was so unexpected that it first alarmed his Hartfield relatives, but he assured them that there was no emergency; everyone in Brunswick Square was well. No, he had some unexpected business in their area and so had driven down on the spur of the moment.

Emma made sure he had a cup of tea and a plate of meat and bread and cheese and apple tart, and told the servants to ready a room. Her father's curiosity, assured that his daughter and grandchildren were healthy, went no further, but Emma and her husband were both certain that there had to be a specific reason for Mr. John Knightley's coming so suddenly to see them. Mr. John Knightley's eyes sparkled with some untold story, but as they understood that it could be something he preferred to convey in private, they all praised Mr. Woodhouse's gruel until the old man went to bed.

"So, John, will you tell us why you are here?" Mr. Knightley asked, pouring them each a glass of wine.

Mr. John Knightley reached into his pocket, took out a silver spoon and passed it to his brother. "Do you recognize this, George?"

Mr. Knightley exclaimed: "What? But I thought it was stolen." He passed the spoon to Emma; she did not know it as well as her husband did, but it looked like a piece from the set at Donwell Abbey.

"It *was* stolen," said Mr. John Knightley.

"Then how have you found it?"

Mr. John Knightley sipped his wine and explained that he was walking with a client along C—Street, where he saw something familiar in a shop window. The shop's reputation was not stainless, but Mr. John Knightley's client had considerable influence in the area, so they went inside. There he identified many more items stolen from Donwell Abbey.

"Someone sold them to the man at the shop?" asked Mr. Knightley.

"Can you guess who it was?" and Mr. John Knightley's eyes twinkled. "It was a man who explained he wanted to sell his mother's silverware."

"Was it a gypsy?" asked Emma. "How could a gypsy fool such a man?"

"No, the merchant swore it was definitely a gentleman. He gave me a description, and I have no doubt who it is." Mr. John Knightley spoke slowly, savoring their anticipation. "Your vicar, Mr. Elton."

"What?" exclaimed Mr. Knightley, while Emma raised her hand to her mouth.

They asked for more particulars; Mr. John Knightley was able to satisfy. They determined from a copy of a bill of sale that the silver had been sold to the merchant the day after Mrs. Bates's funeral.

"You were correct, Emma," said Mr. Knightley. "The Eltons were suffering pecuniary distresses! He must have taken the silver up to London to sell even before anyone knew it was missing."

"And that chest he brought back from London!" Emma cried. "He never had any particular attachment to it. He only said that so he would have a good reason for taking his carriage."

"A chest?" asked Mr. John Knightley. "You know, the merchant said that the seller – or rather the thief – bought an old chest that he had on his premises. But I don't understand what you mean about Elton's carriage, Emma."

"Why don't you explain, my dear," said Mr. Knightley, and he rose to place another log on the fire.

Emma told their brother about the chest; how it had been the excuse for Mr. Elton's taking the carriage to London. Yet it was not very attractive and Mr. Elton had not treated it with any especial interest or respect. "Now we know that it was only a ruse, so that Mr. Elton could take the carriage *to* London without raising suspicion."

"How very elaborate," said Mr. John Knightley coolly. "Why didn't he just pretend to have a cold?"

They all laughed, and Mr. Knightley teased his younger brother that he was obviously better equipped than Elton for a life of crime. Mr. John Knightley admitted that as a lawyer he was accustomed to thinking deviously.

"I owe you a compliment, Emma," said her husband. "I never appreciated the significance of that ugly chest, while you realized immediately that something was wrong."

Emma was happy to be proved right – or at least not entirely wrong – in this instance. "It is a hideous piece of furniture," she said, "not worthy of being appreciated for itself, and Mr. Elton never behaved as if it meant anything to him. I rather expect they decided that Mr. Elton would choose any piece of furniture that suited – good enough for their plan – but that Mrs. Elton must have felt dismay when she saw what he had brought back."

"I'm sure her displeasure was alleviated by all the cash," said Mr. John Knightley coolly.

"Have you been able to retrieve the silver?" was the next question.

Mr. John Knightley assured his brother and his fair sister-in-law that most of the Donwell silver could be retrieved. The proprietor of the shop claimed to be annoyed to learn he had dealt in stolen goods, for Mr. Elton had appeared exceedingly respectable. He was even more irritated to learn that the thief had broken into a household in which the owner was a magistrate and his brother an experienced lawyer. He had set aside most of it, save one or two pieces, which he had already sold to third parties.

"Of course he wants his money back," said Mr. John Knightley.

And that led to the problem of what to do with Mr. Elton.

"We can't have a clergyman who steals from people's houses!" Mr. Knightley proclaimed decisively, while Emma wondered if he had robbed others.

No, such corruption in their vicar was intolerable. "He can hardly preach virtue in his sermons if he is a known thief," said Mr. John Knightley. "Nor will anyone have confidence inviting him into sickrooms if they believe he is planning to pocket a brooch or a spoon."

Emma reminded her husband that Mr. Elton had been seen fingering old Mrs. Bates's golden locket after she died. "The theft at Donwell Abbey was bold – it would make sense if he had attempted smaller thefts earlier."

The next day the two Mr. Knightleys paid an early visit to the Eltons. Emma could not justify going, of course, and besides she was needed by her child and her father, but both her husband and his brother promised her a full account of what transpired.

They first spoke to just Elton alone. The handsome young vicar turned red, and then white as John Knightley laid out the case, explained he had a witness, and even a copy of the bill of sale of the chest from the shop in question.

"He wants his money back," said Mr. Knightley. "At which point he will return my silver to me."

Elton broke down and confessed and threw himself on their mercy. He could not help himself; his crimes were the result of his nagging wife. Augusta – Mrs. Elton – wanted to be first in Highbury. She was irked when she heard of her sister's patronage of the school in Maple Grove; she became shrill when she saw Mrs. Knightley's fine clothes and was told of Mr. Woodhouse's generosity. She conceived of the musical afternoon as a way of establishing herself – she worked very hard to make it a success. But they needed money; they always needed money.

"So is Mrs. Elton involved?" asked Mr. John Knightley.

At this point the vicar hesitated. He obviously did not want to implicate his wife, and Mr. John Knightley was reluctant to press, given that she was a mother with a very young child. Still, more information came out.

"She blames *you* for everything, Emma," said Mr. John Knightley.

"How is this possible? How can *I* be culpable?" asked Emma, because for once she felt no guilt.

"Mrs. Elton is not the most rational of beings," said Mr. Knightley, "and she dislikes you even more than you dislike her, my dear. Envy is the root of the matter. When you were yet unmarried she could enjoy her position as chaperone with respect to you, but ever since we married she has grown more discontent. From money, to your position in Hartfield, to the fact that you are more lovely and more talented than she: the whole situation, which she had no means to overcome. Even your baby is better than hers."

"You only say that because he's your child, too!" said Emma, passing him their son.

"Perhaps I am prejudiced," Mr. Knightley acknowledged, jiggling the little boy, who laughed in delight. "At any rate, Mrs. Elton's jealousy fueled her desire to establish herself as the leader among the matrons of Highbury. At first she wanted to increase her income, and so she speculated with some of her capital. Unfortunately she lost several thousand pounds and their means decreased."

"I had no idea it was so serious."

"It struck her as quite unfair that *you* should be the mistress of the two largest houses in the area, while she – and in most ways she considers herself superior to you – has only one. She wanted to punish you. If she could have, she would have made Elton steal valuables from Hartfield, but Donwell Abbey was easier."

What was to be done with them, became the next point of discussion.

"They are considering emigrating, either to the former colonies in America or down to Australia," said Mr. John Knightley.

Mr. Knightley said, "Mr. Elton would make a fresh start and Mrs. Elton thinks it would give greater scope to her talents."

"It seems suitable," said Emma. "Those places are already full of criminals."

Mr. John Knightley finished his wine, excused himself and went to bed.

"My dear, what about your talents?" Mr. Knightley asked.

"*My* talents?" asked Emma. "Certainly my talents have had plenty of exercise lately."

"Yes, but the dramas are over. The killers have been caught; the locket returned; we may even retrieve the Donwell silver. Mrs. Churchill, the closest you had to an intellectual peer, has departed. Your intimacy with Mrs. Weston has sunk. Even Mrs. Elton, your sparring partner, is planning to leave."

"Perhaps I will take a greater interest in farming, Mr. Knightley."

"Perhaps you will – perhaps you only hope you will. But farming does not often require a lot of imagination."

"You are very kind to be concerned, but it is not necessary. I have my father and you and our son to occupy me, and Jane has promised to correspond. With the crimes committed by the Eltons, Mrs. Weston will no longer feel quite as disgraced, and we will be restored to our former level of intimacy. Perhaps the new vicar – Highbury will need a new vicar – will have a wife worth knowing. And if these things do not amuse me, then I will copy Mrs. Elton, and organize a musical afternoon."

He caught her hand and raised it to his lips. "You are a treasure, my Emma." .

AUTHOR'S NOTE

Jane Austen's *Emma* has been famously described as a detective novel without a body. I always thought this was a little odd because there was a body – Mrs. Churchill – who died at a most convenient point in the novel. The true murderess was actually Jane Austen, but I always wondered if any of the other characters could have played a role in her death. Frank Churchill was certainly one possibility, but almost too obvious. Who else had a motive? Mr. Weston had disliked Mrs. Churchill for years, and might have realized that she was standing in his son's way. I also theorized that he might have done something similar with his first wife, Frank's natural mother, when she died of a lingering illness two decades before.

Here is the inspirational section from Jane Austen's *Emma*:

"An express arrived at Randalls to announce the death of Mrs. Churchill. Though her nephew had had no particular reason to hasten back on her account, she had not lived above six-and-thirty hours after his return. A sudden seizure, of a different nature than anything forboded by her general state, carried her off after a short struggle. The great Mrs. Churchill was no more."

Thirty-six hours would be enough time to kill off someone using a poisonous mushroom, especially the one known as the "death cap," or more formally as *Amanita phalloides,* and causes symptoms consistent with those described in *Emma*. Furthermore, *Amanita phalloides* is common in Britain and could have easily been gathered by Mr. Weston and Mr. Frank Churchill during their visit to Box Hill.

Besides, Emma Woodhouse Knightley, with her tendency to speculate, seems like an ideal detective for a cozy mystery. I apologize to Mr. Weston for blackening his reputation, but as Mr. Knightley once remarked to Mrs. Weston in the original *Emma*:

"…and if Weston had asked me to recommend him a wife, I should have certainly named Miss Taylor."

"Thank you. There will be very little merit in making a good wife to such a man as Mr. Weston."

"Why, to own the truth, I am afraid you are rather thrown away, and that with every disposition to bear, there will be nothing to be borne. We will not despair, however. Weston may grow cross from wantonness of comfort, or his son may plague him."

As some readers may not be that familiar with *Emma*, or may have not read it in a while, I felt it necessary to review quite a bit of that plot. I did what I could to immerse myself in Jane Austen's style and the sentiments her characters expressed in her novels and what she herself expressed in letters and other works and paid homage whenever I could to her style and structure. *Emma*, a romance, opens with the characters reacting to a wedding; *The Highbury Murders*, a mystery, begins with the characters reacting to a death.

I did my best to extrapolate the characters in a manner consistent with Jane Austen's original work. Mr. Knightley is independent, a bit of a free-thinker, and aware that their lifestyle does not offer Emma much scope for developing or using her intellect. I suspect that the sweet but dithering Harriet Smith Martin may actually be suffering from Attention Deficit Disorder. I gave Jane Fairfax an interest in mathematics – in the eighteenth century, great strides had been made, especially in the understanding of probability – which is consistent with her observation in *Emma* about the size of the Maple Grove parish. Mrs. Elton is jealous and vain; Frank Churchill is morally weak. And although I may have cruelly blackened Mr. Weston's character, it was amusing to create a reason for the Churchills having never liked him. This is an homage to Jane Austen's treatment of Mr. Darcy in *Pride and Prejudice*, for Mr. Darcy is also misjudged by nearly everyone in Meryton, simply because they all prefer the company of the far more engaging Mr. Wickham.

Choices with respect to spelling and punctuation were a little awkward. Editions of Jane Austen's novels are not consistent in their treatments; for example, I have seen "Randall's" and "Randalls" and many other variations.

Although I owe the best of *The Highbury Murders* to the genius of Jane Austen, in the end the arrangement and the selection and the flaws are my own.

Victoria Grossack, 2013.

ABOUT THE AUTHOR

Victoria Grossack, besides having devoured all the novels of Jane Austen and greatly enjoying detective stories, is a student of Greek mythology. She is the author, with Alice Underwood, of the Tapestry of Bronze novels:

Jocasta: The Mother-Wife of Oedipus

Children of Tantalus: Niobe & Pelops

The Road to Thebes: Niobe & Amphion

Arrows of Artemis: Niobe & Chloris

Antigone & Creon: Guardians of Thebes

Victoria is also responsible for the column "Creating Fabulous Fiction" at www.writing-world.com

More about Victoria and her novels can be found at www.tapestryofbronze.com